THE ONLY SOUND

IS THE WIND

THE ONLY SOUND

IS THE WIND

Pascha Sotolongo

W. W. NORTON & COMPANY

Independent Publishers Since 1923

Lines from "Tonight I Can Write the Saddest Lines" from *Twenty Love Poems and
a Song of Despair* by Pablo Neruda published by Jonathan Cape. Copyright © W.S.
Merwin, 1969. Reprinted by permission of Penguin Books Limited.

For information about permission to reproduce selections from this book, write to
Permissions, W. W. Norton & Company, Inc.
500 Fifth Avenue, New York, NY 10110

For information about special discounts for bulk purchases, please contact
W. W. Norton Special Sales at specialsales@wwnorton.com or 800-233-4830

Manufacturing by Sheridan
Book design by Beth Steidle
Production manager: Gwen Cullen

ISBN 978-1-324-07644-5 (pbk)

W. W. Norton & Company, Inc., 500 Fifth Avenue, New York, NY 10110
www.wwnorton.com

W. W. Norton & Company Ltd., 15 Carlisle Street, London W1D 3BS

1 2 3 4 5 6 7 8 9 0

Contents

Sustain

THE ONLY SOUND

IS THE WIND

YOU MIGHT THINK THE DESERT DREAMS OF THE SEA, BUT I think deserts dream of other deserts, scorched spaces just like themselves. With them, they don't feel so alien, so bizarre. They don't have the bother of explaining—the way they would with the sea—how it is they're all sand and rock and sagebrush and how the only sound is the wind across the earth.

ⵣ   ⵣ   ⵣ

My back aches. Three minutes is a long time to stand at the sink rinsing rice, but then—the arsenic. When the timer dings, I dump the rice in a sizzling pan and reach in the fridge for a Belgian dark. Gluten free. I have an antibody for most everything. The smell of saffron rises, takes me back to Miami, Mamá's kitchen. In those days the world was good and sweet and I could eat mountains of paella without sprouting the kind of shrimp rash ER doctors term "impressive."

After dinner, I set my plate in the sink and head for the garage. Finally I get to open the box. An eBay buy from a year ago: *Lot of assorted items. Books, toys, etc. Sci-fi geek's fantasy.* Something like that. I don't quite remember anymore. It's been in the garage ever since, waiting out its quarantine. Bedbugs can live up to a year without feeding, and they're immune to cold. Since books are among their favorite haunts, I circled the date on the calendar and—until today—closed my mind to it.

Bending back the cardboard flaps, I see the Spock collection first thing. There are plastic action figures with real clothes, stickers, a coloring book, and a Starfleet Academy Vulcan-language guide—all in great condition. For years, I wanted to marry Spock. We'll find you a nice Cuban boy, Papi would say, maybe someone rich. But I only had eyes for the Vulcan. Which Papi didn't mind, in theory. At least Spock wasn't blond and square jawed. Papi hated those kinds of guys. But then no girl can marry a fiction.

At the bottom of the box, just beneath some goofy *Next Generation* stuff, there is a *Popular Science* magazine from the eighties. I sweep the vacuum over it, page by page, then head inside to peruse. Candles always plunk the cherry on anything enjoyable, so I light one. Soy wax. Lead-free wick. The warm yellow glow lights me up.

Much of the content is funny. An entire month's salary for a VCR. An article about the revolution that is Apple's 32-bit Mac Mini. Others on plastic engines, earth homes, an 88-pound plane. The classifieds are the best, though. There's the Thompson Vocal Eliminator, a machine that removes most of the lead vocals from a standard record and leaves most of the background music untouched. All your favorite songs cleaved like walnuts just for you.

One ad contains a whole block of words so tiny I go get the magnifying glass and turn on another light. The big type reads simply, CLONE AT HOME. Then I hold up the glass and squint:

One clone sent directly to your house. Glitch-free process based on cutting-edge science. Simply take a ¹/₁₆" bundle of hair from whatever you wish to have cloned (human or animal) and mail it to the address below in a well-sealed plastic container. Allow 4–6 weeks processing. All sales final! $350.

After this, the address and a little order form that you're supposed to snip out of the magazine and include with your hair and payment. I guffaw, look for clues it's a joke. But everything about the ad—from the font, to the wording, to the drawing of a fluffy-haired man and his shadowy double—suggests otherwise. Yeah, it's laughable, but not meant to be.

Tossing the magazine aside, I rise, stretch, and head to the kitchen. I'll need a new loaf of gluten-free bread for the week. I've just lined up the five different flours when the phone rings. A coworker trying to rally a few of us for cocktails and mini golf. But there is bread to make, a Target order to place, laundry piling. A whole crop of gray hairs— for which I am too young—waits to be hennaed. I haven't exercised in days. Weariness settles across my shoulders, and I tell her I can't.

She says but Luke will be there and doesn't that make me reconsider. In fact, it does. Luke is tall and lanky, gray-eyed and blond. Sorry, Papi. He's like a thirty-year-old English schoolboy. His fair genes wouldn't stand a chance against my Cuban ones. Our kids would definitely be dark.

No, I say. If I'm going to meet up with Luke socially, I at least want my hair freshly colored. Maybe next weekend, I offer. She groans that I'm no fun. I don't dispute it, hang up the phone, and start in on the bread.

One hundred grams of almond flour, fifty of teff, fifty of millet . . . Just when I get all the dry ingredients mixed, I reach for a paper towel and elbow the whole concoction onto the floor. The metal bowl clangs against hard wood, and a white plume rises around me. I want to cry but curse instead, kicking the bowl across the kitchen, then go to the living room and collapse on the sofa. Tired. Of what, I'm not entirely sure. Just tired. My hand reaches for the phone. Miami. My parents. Only to hear your voice, I'd say. Just hi. But instead I pick up the Spock doll and straighten his tiny blue shirt.

Beside me on the sofa, the *Popular Science*. An idea quivers through my chest like a penny rippling down through water. When it hits bottom, I hop up and go to the porcelain cow bank where I keep all the cash Tío Juan has ever sent me. Each Christmas and birthday for as long as I can remember: a fresh fifty. I fish out seven bills and notice what a good beard Grant has.

I tear out the little form, fill in the blanks—name, address, phone number—and grab a plastic zipper bag from the kitchen. In the bathroom, I stand before the mirror, take a thick bundle of hair in my left hand, and scissor right through it. The long coil plunks softly into the sink. It's far too big. I see this right away. It definitely shows. The laughter comes hard and deep. I'll be mortified in the morning, when stark daylight illuminates the ugly gap, the thick hedge of freshly shorn hair just above my left ear. But for now, it's only funny, funny, and funnier.

Back in the kitchen, I double-check the instructions and notice the asterisk. *Pull hair from scalp or skin.* Shit. So I rip out a few more strands, swap them with the poundage of hair I stupidly cut, stuff everything into the envelope, and stick on five dollars' worth of stamps. Maybe more. I lose track.

Out into the cricket night. The hinge on the mailbox creaks when I open the little door, loud in the empty street. It closes with a satisfying *thunk*, and I go back inside. *That's what I need: a like-minded team of two.*

⸬   ⸬   ⸬

Luke works at the fudge shop near my office building. He has an MFA in fine art and lives with his parents, well, rents the apartment over their garage here in Madison. He tells me this apologetically. I pull my chair closer to the little table we're sharing and nibble the cranberry fudge he's brought. Laughing and complaining over mini golf, my coworkers brandish their putters like weapons. You can't help it if the arts don't pay anything, I tell him. He's preparing to send fifty postcards of his artwork to children's publishing houses.

I never wanted to do commercial art, he says, but how many people get exactly what they want? Anyway, children's books might be fun. He smiles feebly, like he's trying to believe it, and shows me a postcard. On one side, a glossy image of a rooster wearing trousers and a monocle.

Very nice, I say.

I go home thinking about his gray eyes, his limp blond hair, and I'm glad that—just as we were all leaving mini golf—I invited him to lunch. At my house. A bold move for me, but I hate eating out. The stats on restaurant employee hygiene are appalling. Anyway, Luke appeals to me. I glance around the kitchen. He might sit in that chair there, or stand in the doorway there, looking out at the backyard, the decorative grasses' brittle music wafting in through the screen.

But the next day, when the doorbell rings, I regret the whole thing. What if it's too awkward to ask him to remove his shoes? I can't have him bringing all those outside germs inside. My neighbor never wears shoes, the dirty soles of his feet, little black ovals, winking down to the mailbox each day. I'm certain that's why he spent several months laid up last year. A mystery illness, he said. And what if Luke uses my bathroom? He might sleep with two or three girls a week for all I know. Or maybe he spends his spare time at the public library, where bedbugs seem to have set up permanent residence, their eggs sticking to the seat of his pants like sand, sifting off when he sits on my sofa.

More fudge, lemon pistachio this time. Fantastic, I say. I love pistachios. He smiles, kisses my cheek. My eyes flutter as he leans in, but afterwards, I can think of nothing to say. Lunch goes well enough. But he doesn't wash his hands before we eat, and there is a flicker of surprise when I ask him to remove his shoes.

We sit on the back porch watching the wind in the trees, coins of sunlight roving over the grass like spotlights. The beer is nice, and we're feeling awfully cozy. I even think he might kiss me soon. Then he sniffles, coughs, and says he hopes he's not getting a cold, that one of his coworkers has a cold. My head suddenly feels full. I don't need a cold. Colds turn into sinus infections and bronchitis. Bronchitis into pneumonia.

What would I do then? I'm allergic to a whole host of antibiotics, not to mention they decimate gut flora, some of those essential good bacteria now as rare as California condors. And who's to say it's just a cold? Lots of folks think they have colds when they really have COVID, or influenza, or something worse. We are a civilization invaded: drug-resistant bacteria, foodborne illness, antibodies that turn our own flesh against us. People don't know what the hell's going on with them half the time.

Do you feel feverish? I ask.

Nah, he says, just a little tickle in the throat. It's nothing. He's blithe. When he moves closer, my heart sprints. I can't kiss him now. Impossible. I'm no good at bluntness or hurting people's feelings. Lying is my only out, but nothing's coming. He reaches for my hand. Right away I feel it. His skin is clammy. He's percolating *something*. I'm just about to feign a bathroom trip when the doorbell rings and I spring from my chair.

It's delivery, a giant box the size of a coffin on a dolly the delivery guy can barely manage. It's a big one, he says, straining to pull it up the two steps into my foyer.

Are you sure it's for me? I ask. I get packages all the time but can't recall ordering anything this big and heavy.

Yeah. He hands me the paper. Ana Delgado, right?

I nod. Then a signature pad. My hand scrawls out some lines, and he tells me to have a nice day. The door closes. Air pressure modulates. With its cardboard smell, its intrusive size, the box is most definitely here, just as Luke and I are here. But now, instead of looking at me and reaching for my hand, Luke stands in the doorway between foyer and living room staring at it. The pressure of his inviting face and potential germs—blissfully vaporized. We are a triangle: the strongest shape.

What is it? he asks.

I wish I knew. One of my knees cracks when I bend down to examine the label. CLONE AT HOME, it says.

I stand but my legs shake, and the only thing I can think to say is I just started my period, a strange lie for me. I'm not one to talk about such things, especially to guys I kind of like. But it tumbles out and the effect is pretty good. He fumbles and stretches around the box like he can't get to his shoes quickly enough.

Sorry, I say, bad timing.

That's okay. Just get to feeling better. Do you need anything before I go? He sniffles again and his eyes are glassy. Maybe it's allergies. He looks like he might lean in for a hug or, worse, a kiss, so I position myself with the box between us and place a hand low on my stomach.

Sorry again, I say.

Another time, though? He looks hopeful, beautiful.

For sure.

As we're exchanging pleasantries, taking our leave in that way humans have of mixing sincerity with artifice, a question rises: *What is it?* A mannequin? A robot? A giant puppet? I lock the front door, push the box into the living room, and sit on the floor beside it. Ear to cardboard. Silence. No breathing. No movement. I even give the box a good shove, then swiftly lean in to listen again. Still nothing. A murder of crows drops into the backyard, their shrill calls loud against the stillness. Black wings flash in my peripheral vision. I grab the box cutter, my hands trembling. Tape, cut. Flaps, loose. My fingers, lifting. Revealed, a sleeping woman. Just like me.

*   *   *

The clone and I sit in the living room regarding each other. Neither of us speaks. My breathing has become wheezy, asthmatic, and not even the rescue inhaler has helped much. She blinks and looks around apprehensively, her dark eyes big and shocked. Just like mine, I imagine. Something startles the crows and they lift en masse, blooming like a mushroom cloud. Our heads turn, and for a moment we are three again, the pressure easing just enough that I find my voice.

So . . . do I *own* you?

She shrugs and asks if you can really own another person.

Are you a person, then? I ask.

She shrugs again but looks injured.

She twitches her foot, and I try not to stare at every inch of her. Right down to the gap in her hair, she is just like me. The clone keeps glancing over, and when our eyes meet, I feel dizzy, waves of nausea mounting. I shake my head. So this is how it all culminates—the strain of modern life, the solitude, a destination I never imagined. Me lying on the sofa. Her sitting in the chair. The wind rising outside.

Can I bring you some peppermint tea? she asks. It might help with the nausea.

Okay, I answer. Thank you.

*   *   *

Though I feel healthy enough, I call in sick the next day. For the first few hours I try to locate a phone number, a website, anything at all about Clone at Home. There is nothing. As far as I can tell, they don't exist anymore. Maybe they never did. The address they used to occupy now belongs to a frozen yogurt shop.

In the kitchen, the clone makes tea and toast. She moves through the space like she knows it, deftly opening just the right drawers and cabinets. Eventually she sets a cup before me, chocolate Earl Grey with two ounces of almond milk and six grams of sugar. That's exactly how I like it, I tell her.

Me too. She smiles.

The clone seems to recall nothing of her recent life, neither the people who cloned her nor how she came to my door. Still, a deep and familiar history lies within her. Her long-term memories are mine. I tell her the first half of a childhood story. She tells the rest: falling overboard on the Jungle Cruise. During lunch we even laugh over the memory of Papi getting angry and punching a bag of Fritos, little tan shingles spraying up, then landing softly as magnolia leaves across his lap.

I watch her bite into her toast, chew the way I do, dimples blinking in her cheeks. Are her morals the same as mine? Will she slit my throat in the night and take my place in the world? Is she really a pod person from outer space? The tea is hot, so she blows, sips tentatively, glances at me as she swallows.

How do I know I can trust you?

How do I know I can trust *you*? she replies.

I shrug. You just can. I know what I'm capable of. I know I wouldn't hurt you.

Well, that's me too. The fact is, tu eres mi otro yo. How can you not be as precious to me as my own life?

Somewhere a dog barks. Toast crunches. Okay, I finally say.

I'd imagined a clone would do all the crummy things I didn't want to: cleaning the bathroom, washing dishes, laundry, grocery shopping, even going to work for me on Mondays so I could have three-day weekends. Clearly I hadn't thought the matter through. So the clone and I form a plan, something more equitable than my original ideas. For now, I'll go to work. She'll stay home and take care of the house. Then, after a while, we'll switch.

We spend the afternoon baking. After dinner, we play games. Being with her, it turns out, is just as easy as being alone, only not lonely, so it's better. She washes her hands at all the right times. She likes what I cook. She understands everything I say. Feel. Am. When I'm able to let my guard down, a peculiar sense of relief fans across my brain like a limpid wave. I feel hydrated.

The clone asks if I can stay home tomorrow too, so I explain how it is at the office. That no one takes time off. A sick day here and there at the most. Taking vacation is the best way to end your career.

Why? she asks.

Because Americans live to work, I say. Our jobs own us. The digital archive of a major midwestern insurance company owns me.

But you look tired, she says.

I am. Everyone is. Desperately. But we have no choice.

She nods and pads off to the bathroom. I clear a few last dishes and pull out the sofa bed. Outside lights are next, but I find she's already done that. When I turn into the hall, I see a crisp rectangle of bathroom light, the door mostly open. Something about the silence makes me pause. What's she doing so quietly? Shouldn't the water be running by now? I draw near and ask if everything's okay. A flutter of movement in the mirror, dark hair, a hand reaching, but she quickly shuts the door and says she's fine. She'll be out in a minute.

When I get home from work, the house is spotless and a big pot of chicken soup steams on the stove. Garlic, onion, saffron. Hey! I'm home, I call out.

From the back of the house, her voice, Oh good. Dinner's just ready.

Oddly, a box of fudge on the dining table. Rocky road. Where'd this come from? I ask.

She rounds the corner. Your friend Luke was here. He said he thought he'd take a chance on your being home since you were out sick yesterday. I didn't know what to do, so I invited him in for a sandwich.

Oh.

He's nice, isn't he? Do you like him?

Kind of.

He likes you.

And you, apparently.

Okay, he likes *us*. She draws her hair back from her face, holds it at the nape of her neck as she speaks. Is that a problem?

I don't know. I mean, for now, I guess, if we're careful, we could manage. But what if things get serious? Eventually, he'd have to know we were three. Trouble is, three always become two.

She nods, thoughtful. Worried. Like I feel.

Over dinner, she tells me about Luke's visit. I need to know all that transpired, I say, or it could be weird next time I see him.

She knots her eyebrows, looks down as she chews, thinking hard. We made a date for this Friday. Is that okay? You're going to dinner and the museum, that graphic art exhibit.

I hate eating out, I say, moaning. I wish you hadn't done that.

I hate eating out too, but I couldn't figure how to say no. He was so nice and all.

Yeah. Drat.

On the refrigerator, something new: a magnet. It's E.T. holding a pot of flowers, his chest glowing orangey gold. What's that?

She looks up. I walked down to that thrift shop today and found it there.

I wish I could have gone with you, I say. That would have been fun.

She smiles. Me too.

Did Luke go?

Yeah, we strolled down there together after lunch. He only stayed a few minutes. Then he had to get to work.

I search the clone's face for signs of artifice or malice, then realize she is *all* artifice—by virtue of her existence.

When next I see Luke, he smiles, takes my hand, leans in to kiss my cheek. The fudge shop is empty, and he smells like milk and vanilla. Then he slides over to kiss me on the lips. What's obvious is—this isn't a first kiss. When I flinch, surprised, he draws back and looks perplexed.

Not okay?

I smile. No, it's fine. You just caught me off guard.

He pushes long bangs away from his forehead. I've been dreaming about that kiss at the thrift shop all week, he says. Couldn't wait to try it again. Too eager, I guess. He laughs and ducks his head in a moment of self-reproach. Like he's a goofball.

No, you're fine, I insist. It was a wonderful kiss. I'm really looking forward to tonight.

He sniffles and smiles, encouraged. Me too. Another sniffle.

You must have hay fever. The weed pollen's high.

Yeah, he says. I think I do.

The bell over the door clangs and a family wanders in, kids chattering and bouncing as they rush to the counter and begin the serious work of selecting a flavor. I smile and wave, mouth, See you at seven, as I back out the door. I should return to work, but somehow, I can't. So I call in, claim a relapse of my Monday illness, and drive home.

The house smells like cardamom and lamb. Sizzling meat and the chorus of "Down Under" fill the kitchen. On the refrigerator, another E.T. magnet. This time he holds up a glowing finger, his giant blue eyes glistening like alpine lakes. The clone wears shorts and rainbow leg warmers.

Another thrift store buy?

Yeah. She smiles. I went alone.

I know. I just saw him.

She looks down at the rainbows. Do they look stupid?

No, I mean, they're fine for inside. You heated them up, I hope?

In the dryer. One hundred twenty-five degrees. Bedbugs, dead bugs. She clamps a lid on the stew pot and slides it from the burner into the oven, sets the timer and turns to me. You're early, she says.

I know. I turn down the music. I need to talk to you. We sit, and outside, wind chimes tinkle. Listen, why didn't you tell me you and Luke kissed at the thrift store? I should have known that, don't you think?

She studies her thumbnail. I guess I was embarrassed.

Why?

Because he seemed sick, and I knew I shouldn't have let

him kiss me. What if I get what he has? I could give it to you, and we'd both be sick. It was stupid. I should have been stronger. The clone looks distressed, picking at her cuticle, the corners of her mouth folding downward.

I think he has hay fever, I say.

Oh good. She looks up.

Yeah.

⊪   ⊪   ⊪

The local news details several recent break-ins. Broad daylight. Armed robbers. Brazen, the reporter calls them. Then a segment on how to stay safe in your home. We might need to consider that, the clone says, meaning our back door. We need one of those deadbolts that's keyed on both sides. She makes little turning motions with her hands. That way, if they break the glass, they can't just flip the deadbolt and waltz in. Her eyebrows rise as she speaks.

And maybe a camera out front, I say. Even a good fake one.

It's getting out of control, she says.

I agree. A neighbor one house over was robbed last year, and the following morning, my gate was open. The robbers had been in my backyard, sizing up my house, maybe reaching for my door when an unexpected sound or light startled them away. I was that close to danger. We'll call tomorrow, I say.

No, she says. Tomorrow's Saturday.

Monday then.

She grabs a notepad and starts a to-do list. With every item she adds, something inside me eases, like she's lifting bricks from a basket strapped to my back.

I eat a small dinner before I have to leave to get Luke. This is partly because I won't eat much at the restaurant and partly because the clone's lamb smells ridiculously good. It's my recipe, of course, but I rarely have time to make it. Sitting here like this, the pot of lamb between us, a candle glimmering, the television prattling away but her there to absorb some of it—I'd like to just stay home. Nestle down into the sofa, watch a movie, rest. But I consider Luke and rise to dress—then think better of it. Would you like to go with him tonight instead of me?

Her eyes widen. Qué?

Spanish. I miss the sound of it and, for a moment, close my eyes. I mean it, I say. You can drive, can't you? His car's not running.

She nods. I can drive. But I don't especially want to go.

You don't?

She shakes her head.

Well, neither do I. I mean I do, but it almost doesn't seem worth the trouble. Is that just sad?

She smiles. Maybe? She finally relents. Okay. I'll go.

$$\text{\textbardbl} \qquad \text{\textbardbl} \qquad \text{\textbardbl}$$

I lie on the sofa twisting a Rubik's Cube, the television flashing green and blue. Like the magnets, the cube is new. The clone microwaved it to kill any bedbugs, and now, in places, the plastic has melted. But it still turns. Part of me regrets staying home, wishes I were with Luke, or with the clone. There is definitely some jealousy, though whether of him or of her, I can't say. The kettle whistles and I pour the steaming water into a cup, bounce a teabag. The clone has baked lime and guava galletas—Mamá's recipe. The taste is so like home I grab three more and settle back onto the sofa. As the intense sweet-tartness of the cookies tingles through my cheeks, I realize the clone is the only Cuban I know outside of Miami. And Miami is more than a thousand miles away. Just as I'm drifting off, the sound of a key in the lock. The door opens.

You're early, I say.

I know.

What happened?

The exhibit was stupid.

De verdad?

Sí. Muy. There were all these really macabre things—you know—emaciated, eviscerated, mutilated.

Todos?

No, some of it was just skeletons with ram horns and giant chi-chis.

Did Luke like it?

He seemed to, but it was hard to tell. He'd taken a Bena-dryl and was kind of walking dead. I think he even started to drool at one point. This with a laugh. Anyway, I kept wishing I were here with you, she says, removing her shoes, then trailing off to wash her hands. Actually, I'm going to get changed and washed for bed, she calls to me. I'm tired.

Okay, I yell, glad she's home, a little smile rising from somewhere deep inside. Then she's coming back down the hallway. Fast. When she turns the corner, she looks alarmed.

What was that? she asks. Holding still. Listening.

What was what? I whisper.

This time we both hear it, a shuffling on the back porch. Silence. Then an explosive bang at the door and the euphonic tinkle of broken glass. Something has shattered the window just above the deadbolt. When a breeze lifts the curtain, I see the hole and around it a radiating web of cracks.

Shit! one of us says. The clone grabs the bat from the front closet and I pick up my phone, ready to dial but staring at the deadbolt, the open space through which someone could simply reach. How easily our lives are upended.

I'm sorry. A familiar voice whimpers. I tripped.

I look at the clone. Is that Luke?

She nods.

It *is* Luke, the voice says.

I go to the door, intercept the flapping curtain and peek out. Luke is just getting to his feet, a reddish whelp rising on his forehead.

Why are you here? I ask.

I was dropping something off, he says, leaning down to speak through the opening like he's placing an order.

Why didn't you come to the front door?

I brought you a pot of flowers. See? Like that E.T. magnet you bought. I wanted to leave it here for a surprise. Near Luke's feet, the pot has split into two distinct shards, dirt and flowers bleeding out.

I turn the lock, feel the weight and clink as the metal bolt retreats from the strike plate. Luke passes through the open door, a blur of blond hair, white shirt, dark pants.

The clone's voice hits me first, high pitched, panicky. Ana! What are you doing?

I turn to find Luke's face nearly as stricken as the clone's. I gasp. I forgot, I say to the clone, holding her gaze, meaning it, but also hoping she understands I might have done the same even if I'd remembered.

Twins! Luke says.

I nod, lie.

I didn't know.

Oh.

I mean, even the same hairstyle.

You better sit down, I say. You've got a huge knot. I'll get an ice pack. You can take it with you.

I can't even tell you two apart, he continues, holding the ice to his head. To the clone he says, So you're the one I went out with tonight.

She nods.

I can tell by the outfit. He looks at me, then back at the clone. Honestly? This is kind of intense. I don't know if it's cool or just . . . weird. He bobs his head, negotiating the strain.

The clone and I watch as Luke passes the ice from one hand to the other when the cold gets unbearable. Every time he adjusts, the frozen gel makes a gelatinous *glup* sound. Through the broken window, the chimes resonate, and far away, a hint of thunder.

I'm sorry about the door, Ana. I think I was off kilter from the Benadryl. I'll pay of course. Hey. Wait. He stands. Looks at the clone again. So you're not Ana?

The clone looks at me. I'm Ana, I say.

But then who are you? Luke demands of the clone. I've been calling you Ana.

That's okay, the clone says. Don't worry about it.

What's going on with you two? Are you playing a joke on me or something? To his credit, he's more incredulous than irritated, his gray eyes widening, his mouth slightly open.

No, I say. I wish I could explain. But please understand this is no joke. Silence. Maybe we better call it a night. Do you need a ride?

No, I drove my dad's car. I'm fine. Just a little bump.

It's a big bump, I say.

Okay, he replies with a laugh, just a big bump.

What about the Benadryl?

It's fading, he says, and clears his throat. Can I say something? The cold pack casts a shadow across his face, like a visor.

I nod. The clone nods.

I really like you. His eyes move back and forth between us. Then he drops his arm, studies the ice, his forehead blanched, blood driven back by cold. He's deliberating. The clone moves closer to me, so close I feel the heat of her arm next to mine.

Maybe we could work something out, he finally manages. I don't fully understand what's going on here, but I'm a pretty chill guy. Maybe something could—I don't know—be figured out. He peeks almost shyly through his bangs as he speaks.

Thunder again. I glance at the clone. Her profile in this light, at this moment, is unrecognizable. Each slope and curve a revelation. Her dark brows sit low, and her left cheek dimples as she tightens and releases her jaw. Considering—I suppose— Luke's proposition. My ears begin to ring. Slowly, too slowly it seems, the clone turns toward me, her black eyes meeting, holding mine. Something passes between us then, an unspoken word maybe, a decision. I'm not sure what it is, but I feel it just as if she'd handed me a book or a plate.

The clone turns back to Luke and says, I'm so tired. Just so tired.

Me too, I say.

Luke's shoulders round forward. Then he ducks his head once, like he's resigned, shifts toward the door, and apologizes again for the window. Thanks for this, he says, waving the cold pack. He is beautiful and luminous moving into the darkness.

Be careful, the clone and I call out together, like we planned it.

He was bleeding a little, the clone says after he's gone.

Yep, I reply. I noticed that too.

It didn't drip, did it?

I don't think so.

◊   ◊   ◊

The water runs in the bathroom. I stack dishes, wipe up crumbs, and make sure the stove is off. The back door looks good as new, with a keyed deadbolt on both sides now. I feel glad every time I see it.

The clone is washing up early tonight. We spent the whole day together. A sensation of being in Miami, of being a kid again, kept washing over me. Everything easy and familiar. Everything in shorthand. We took a picnic lunch to the park, but there were bees, so we moved to the car. The clone understood it all: the risk, the worry, the fatigue. I didn't have to explain a thing. Sometimes I thought of Luke. Not often. My growing need to be with the clone surprises me. It should be tedious to be with yourself all the time, but it isn't. It isn't exactly being with yourself, either.

Only two sick days left.

I start down the hall toward the bathroom, its familiar rectangle of light slicing through the dark. Except for a tiny trickling sound, it's strangely quiet. Nervous sparks stutter across my skin. Silly, I think. When I get to the door, I look in, start to speak. The clone stands before the mirror. Where her eyes should be, empty sockets gape. They are the color of dragon fruit. In her left hand, two brown eyes, obviously synthetic. In her right hand, a little squeeze bottle. With a steady pressure, she's squirting a clear solution over the eyes, humming lightly.

My gasp makes her pivot toward me. Ana? she calls. Are

you okay? But I am already in the living room, switching on lights, pacing in circles, a heavy vase in my hand. In the other, the phone. When she rounds the corner, her eyes are back, looking as natural and real as my own.

I'm sorry, she's saying. I should have known that would upset you. I should have explained.

You're a *cyborg*? I blurt out, angry.

Just the eyes. The eyes never develop correctly. So they give us these. Bionic. They need lots of lubrication, though. You know, from the constant movement. Otherwise I wouldn't take them out. It's okay. I'm not a machine.

She has no soul. But what I say is, Can you prove it?

She considers for a minute, sits down on the floor and rubs her hand. Will you bring me a sharp blade and some alcohol?

I nod and soon return, set the items on the coffee table. An image of her using the blade against me flashes across my mind, the clone rising up as my life bleeds into the carpet. But if that's the plan, why wait until now? She swabs her palm, then, without even pausing, draws the blade across her skin, a red smile forming in its wake. When she holds up her hand for me to see, she looks like a child, hopeful, pleading, pleased. See? Blood. Just like you.

The one tissue I've brought isn't enough, so I go for more, return with a fat wad, press it against her palm until the bleeding stops. The warmth of her skin, her blood, radiates into my fingers. Can you remember anything else they told you? I ask. Any other surprises coming my way?

No. She shakes her head. That's it. The rest of me is just as normal as you are.

Can I see?

She stands and begins unbuttoning her shirt, slides off her

pants, methodically undressing until there is nothing left but a body as familiar as my own. Same long limbs, same olive brown skin, same belly. For a moment there is only the sound of our breathing. Then my arm twitches. My hand reaches toward her, and I trace a trembling finger along the curve of her hip. Her flesh prickles. She's cold, so I take off my sweat-shirt and pull it over her head, straighten the mess I've made of her hair.

It's still me, she says.

We hug then, and it's like hugging someone you love intensely but haven't seen in ages, or with whom you've been angry but are now reconciled. One of us smells like violets.

I'll probably call in sick tomorrow.

On the sofa, we get drowsy, laughing over a memory of our first time baiting a hook with real live worms. Nine years old, I say.

No, eight, she corrects.

Papi said it was time we did it ourselves. We caught a flounder that day. Devil fish, someone said, a cousin trying to freak us out.

On the television, a recall of canned tuna. She grabs the notepad and writes it down. We'll check tomorrow, she says.

I nod, considering the cans in the pantry. Could be a little stack of botulinal death. And beyond the pantry, more deaths await. Formaldehyde off-gassing. Hormones in the plastic. I know the risks of being alive. Still, fear eludes me tonight. Out here in the living room, with the distant chimes clattering in the dark, we are two against it all.

SAD BIRD

THE BIRDS ARE DRUNK AGAIN, WORSE THAN LAST YEAR. A premature frost caused the juniper berries to ferment early, before the cedar waxwings and robins had a chance to wing south for winter. Now they're all boozy and flying at crazy angles into cars and living room windows. My neighbor, Xavier, comes over every morning to give me his dead bird report: two by the trash can, two by the garage door, one on the hood of his car.

"Pobrecitos," I say.

"Pobrecitos," he echoes, and pats my shoulder.

During the days, when I am vacuuming or dusting, their vivid inert bodies catch my eye through windows. And if there's a breeze, the fairy-soft down of their chests and bellies quivers, suggests there is life there, but then I watch and wait and am disappointed. The ornithologist on the midday news said they can't coordinate their movements, not on the ground, not in the air. Most, he explained, are merely tipsy, but now and again some birds overdo it. That's how he put it: they *overdo* it, almost like he was judging them.

When Itzel comes home, I feed her arroz con huevos with salsa and relay the latest news from the television. She has seen the dead birds, of course—everyone in town has—and nods impassively as I fill her in. I finally settle into my seat at our table when she asks if there's avocado, so I get up, slice one, sprinkle it with lime, and set it down beside her. I lean in for a kiss too, but she's just taken a big bite, so I laugh and say, "Later."

In the placid semi-light of our kitchen, Itzel's chewing is audible. Crunchy eggs. "Sorry," I say, a wave of heat dampening my hands. "They got away from me."

"They're fine," she says, but grinds through the hard edges with incredulous eyes.

Years ago, when we first came to Oregon, Itzel and I agreed to focus on her career—she's the ambitious one—so I take care of the house and do the cooking. This way Itzel can devote all her energy to advancing at work, to her book especially. She works hard to support us, rising early and often laboring into the night while I dust the bookshelves or bake bread. Maybe our arrangement sounds unenlightened, but I don't mind it. I've never wanted much more from life than to love and be loved.

Decent eggs—that was my one part to play in the day's clockwork, and I blew it.

"It's very sad about the birds," I say . . . because I haven't been able to stop thinking about them, even when I should turn my mind to eggs and the way their sizzling quiets when they overcook. I sink my fork into a bit of white that's still tender. The brown edges don't bother me, but I'm hardly hungry and eat only to avoid waste. Through the kitchen blinds, I notice a new body under the Japanese maple. "Very sad,"

I can't help repeating, but Itzel only grunts, so I try again. "Remember that nest of robins last spring? Out back?"

She nods and nudges the eggs aside, resorts to a meal of rice and avocado.

I slide my own avocado onto her plate. "The parents were tireless," I say. "Remember?"

"I do," she says.

By the time their young left the nest, the adults looked so scruffy and thin we joked they had the mange, funny because birds can't get mange. Under the table I blot my hands with a paper napkin, sandwiching it like a prayer. Maybe it shouldn't matter this much, a bunch of dead, drunk birds, but I need Itzel to understand why it does. I need her to agree with me that something precious is slipping away.

"You think birds feel love?" I try to sound casual because sometimes, when she has a lot on her mind, these kinds of questions exasperate her.

Itzel looks at me and swallows. Instead of smiling (I was hoping she'd smile), she taps my knuckle with the tine of her fork. "They just do what they're programmed to do, Paloma. Nothing more."

"Uh-huh," I reply, but her word seems wrong. They're not robots. I've seen the blood that comes when their bodies break. It's not my way to argue, so I say "Uh-huh" again but finish with, "It's still sad."

"Radical empathy," she says between bites. Her mouth makes nice shapes when she chews.

My head tilts into a question.

"You," she says, "you practice radical empathy. It's sweet, but save some for later."

I am about to reply that you don't need to save up empathy,

that it's always at the ready, like laughter, when Itzel thanks me for dinner, brushes my hand with her fingertips, and leaves the room. Already I hear the ruffle of papers, the squeaky desk drawer.

The dishes need doing, but I stay at the table reading the Rorschach of our plates. Mine so empty it looks clean but for the oil film and a few red pepper flakes. Itzel's full of food I'll force down cold for breakfast. My parents, at the dinner table, lingered to laugh and carry on, my father scooping up seconds of whatever my mother had cobbled together. We were guaji-ros, but always laughing, always something ticklish and bright perching in our hearts. Happy peasants—I know the trope—but I can't help who we were.

✧ ✧ ✧

I keep the coffee warm for Xavier's visit, grab a jacket, and head outside hoping to discover the trouble has peaked. It hasn't. Pulling on a pair of latex gloves, I begin gathering the bodies, laying them in a felt-lined shoebox I will later bury. Xavier folds his in brown paper bags and deposits them in the trash, but that was never an option for me. From the first dead bird, I've felt the need to honor their passing in some small way. Yes, they're only birds, but that doesn't make their death meaningless. As ridiculous as it might sound, I think they appreciate my burying them: tender fingertips smoothing their ruffles, pleating their wings.

Long hours of death have stiffened one, but the others are still supple and drape across my hand like velvet. From a stand of distant junipers, trills and chirps improve the morning air.

"I've got five this morning," Xavier calls over the fence.

"Three," I reply. All waxwings this time. They are gorgeous birds: brown at the head shading imperceptibly to gray halfway down the back, that blush of yellow on the breast and brighter yellow at the tail tip. Several crimson spots of blood, too. Last week, I had mostly robins, but I'm partial to waxwings. Close by, one calls, the sound so high pitched I blink away tears. Poor uncoordinated things. Poor drunk birds.

"There's coffee," I say to Xavier, now peering over my shoulder at my Puma size 8 box of death. He smells like Old Spice.

"Sounds good," he says. "You're putting them in a shoebox, I see."

"I have to," I say.

He says, "Yes, yes," and goes inside.

When the lid thunks into place, the toll is four. Any more and I'd have to scrounge up a second shoebox. "I won't be long," I say to the dead ones, and set them by the back door.

╪   ╪   ╪

Steam uncoils from our cups and Xavier watches me. We've talked the bird crisis down to nil, so I rise to refill his coffee, which is also a way to occupy the silence.

"Have you been eating enough? You look thin." His eyes grow big when he says this, and he gives my arm a little squeeze. Excitable and about fifteen years my senior, Xavier reminds me of all the men in my family. They have the same Moorish eyes. I am drawn to him. I know this already. When he touches me, I feel something I shouldn't.

"I'm eating fine."

"Are you anxious? Anxiety runs the flesh right off. Your

heart speeds up, and the body just"—he gestures broadly and makes a *whoosh* sound.

"I'm okay."

"You and Itzel having problems?" His face goes bland whenever he says her name.

"That's a pretty personal question," I say with a laugh, because it is, but this doesn't really bother me. I knew he'd get to Itzel. He always does.

Xavier snorts. He's dramatic that way. "You should be with a man," he says, and throws up his hands when I draw breath to protest. "I know, *I know!* I'm an ass to say it." He rises and begins rifling through the cabinets. He has told me this before, that I'm too pretty to be with a woman, that I just haven't met the right man yet. Old-guard stuff, and I should hate or at least snub him for it. Instead I shake my head. If Itzel knew he said these kinds of things, she'd be furious at both of us. Especially me.

Xavier sets down a plate of cookies and pours cream in my coffee. He has fanned the shortbreads in an elegant semicircle, pretty as a peacock's tail. The sight makes me want to cry.

"Eat first, then cry if you must," he says.

"Can I do both at once?"

"Only if you want hiccups."

I laugh, but he's serious. It's all very warm and weird, and I wonder what I'm doing. Xavier is old, I tell myself. He's a man, I tell myself, a bit of a chauvinist too. And most of all, he's not Itzel. I am loyal, an actual living monogamist. Love mated Itzel and me, and that's for life.

Mud has caked on the shovel, so I grab the spade and begin scraping. From here, near the house, the yard looks fine. No sign that out by the back fence a new cemetery mars the otherwise pristine sod. Three little graves so far. Today's will make four. When the shovel is clean, I take it to the grave site and return for the birds. They could almost be sleeping, though only sick or injured birds sleep on their sides. Walking toward the fence, I raise the shoebox high overhead and breathe a prayer for the birds' resurrection. Itzel would find me ludicrous. For that matter, so would Xavier. But in this moment, I want nothing more than for every one of them to blink, shake their heads, and wing into the sky. Me and my empty box gaping after their mounting silhouettes.

Clay in the soil makes the digging hard, but I can't get sloppy. I don't want Itzel to notice what I've done back here. Not that she would rage if she knew. Silence is more her style, but it makes me uneasy when she gets that way. In the spring, I'll sow seed over the bare patches while she's at work. This is a fine plan, but amid the thwacking of the shovel and my own panting, something begins to bother me: a thought, no, a feeling. Guilt. The smeary dirt, the flimsy shoebox, even the felt lining strike me now as shabby and base. I had meant to consecrate, not disdain, their ruined bodies.

From Xavier's yard I hear raking. He's whistling, too, though I can't catch the tune. I look for the sun, but the morning mist has yet to burn off. My watch says 11:30. Itzel comes home around four. There is time, so I abandon the hole, return the shoebox to the patio, and hurry inside to get cleaned up.

⸾ ⸾ ⸾

I'm rinsing rice for dinner when Itzel walks in, hangs up her keys, and tells me we're hosting a party.

In the five years we've lived in this house, we've only had

one social gathering. Three of Itzel's friends from art school came for a weekend. Itzel went to get them from the airport and returned sooner than expected, or maybe I lost track of time. They all walked in to find me lying on the living room floor eating Fritos and listening to the 1975 Rush album, *Fly by Night*. Not that I am especially a fan. I wasn't even alive in the seventies. But when I was a teenager, I came upon the album in a thrift store and fell deeply in love with the cover: that glaring snowy owl, its wings held menacingly aloft, its enormous feet fluffy with down and fierce of talon. I bought it but couldn't afford a record player and never got around to listening to it until the day Itzel's friends arrived. I'd been cleaning out the guest room when I came across it and just had to have a listen on Itzel's phonograph. She only buys vinyl. Authenticity is important to her.

You wouldn't think it mattered so much, but it did. Itzel laughed it off in the moment but later, after her friends were asleep, conveyed in taut whispers how disappointing that was for her, how she'd told her friends all about me: this Miami Cuban girl who dances salsa like a native and could have walked right out of Victor Manuel's *La Gitana Tropical*. "Rush?" she said. "Isn't that a skinny-white-guy-hair band from the eighties?"

I shrugged, but it was dark.

"If I thought that were really you," she continued, "obviously I wouldn't complain. I just think you misrepresented yourself in an important moment."

At the time, I didn't understand what important moment Itzel meant, and once her friends were gone, it felt silly to raise the matter again, but I know her better now. For Itzel, everything must orchestrate toward success, every facet of her life, including me. I don't know how or why impressing her art friends with my authentic Cuban-ness figured in her plans, but it did. And I'm certain she meant well. Both of us grew up poor, but Itzel's poverty haunts and drives her in ways all her own. She's determined we'll want for nothing essential, by which she means food, clothing, shelter, health care. Those less tangible essentials can wait, she thinks. Some nights, when we're falling asleep, she turns to me and whispers about imper- manence. "Just for now, Loma, this push," she says. "Not much longer. Then I won't be so busy. We'll have time together, maybe take a long vacation."

"I know," I say. "I can't wait."

Now, she wants to try again. "Nothing fancy," Itzel says, just a small group of her colleagues. But Itzel's nothing fancy is always beyond my ken. I didn't know how to eat an artichoke until a few months ago, kept chewing and chewing those wretched leaves—like window screen—until Itzel demon- strated the proper way. To my mind, anything that isn't beans and rice or sandwiches conspires to reveal what a rube I am, guajiro through and through. And the conversation will be arty and pretentious, intolerable really. Even Itzel will com- plain. Sometimes I think she dislikes her colleagues more than I do.

"So why have them over?" I ask.

"Ray knows an editor," she says. Itzel's nearly finished writing her book on the Cuban Vanguardia. "Also, to show you off," she says. "Mi *Gitana Tropical*." Whenever Itzel calls me this, I know she's feeling sentimental, but for me it only recalls the Rush incident and starts a nervous tingling in my toes, like I'm about to fall from a great height. I know the painting—a giclée of it hangs in her office—but do not see the resemblance. I'm not pretty like that. My eyes are smaller, my nose bigger, my lips thinner. Still, it seems to make her happy to view me this way, so I don't protest.

"When?" I ask, the starchy rice water finally running clear.

"Next weekend."

"So soon?" I feel my face flush.

"Why? Do you have something going on?" She asks like she knows I can't possibly. It's a fair point. I'm a homemaker, busy yet solitary, but that doesn't mean I have nothing going on.

Out back, still in the shoebox, my birds wait placidly for their graves, for the better coffins I have promised. Beneath my side of our bed, I have stashed a bag of supplies: beads, silk tassels, feathers, needles, and yarn. It was thrilling to sneak off to the craft store and secrete away my booty before Itzel got home. She's a horrible snob about crafting, views it as little more than glue and glitter. She doesn't say this outright, but I know how she feels. If she found me crafting again, it would be worse than Rush.

When we first met, I crafted all the time, and Itzel seemed to find it charming, even said she saw talent in my projects. That's how she convinced me to trade crafting for art classes, but I never liked them and soon stopped going. The creative part of me withered, and I don't recall regarding this as a great loss at the time, but I already suspect the fullness of what I feel now—after fingering only a few beads and sequins—would be difficult to give up again.

◈   ◈   ◈

The air has deadened, and the junipers look bald without their blue-black berries. From what I can tell, the birds devoured the last of them several days ago. Xavier hasn't found a single body in two days, and neither have I. Even the news said the disturbance is over. The only remaining testament to the birds' intemperance is the stubborn purple droppings on cars and cement.

And I guess the timing is good because Itzel's get-together is upon me, and there is much to do. No more time for bird coffins, bird funerals, bird sadness. I need to get this right. Itzel scheduled the party for a Friday evening, so I'm alone in my preparations. Last night she helped with cleaning and will come home early today with most of the food. Still, there is guacamole to make and those lime galletas she'd have me bake every single weekend because she loves them that much. On the dining table, a tumble of flowers waits to be arranged in a manner lovely but not precious—Itzel's directions—though the distinction eludes me. If she were here, I could at least tell by her expression if she approved of the way everything was turning out. That would be a comfort.

Through the living room window, I survey the modest expanse of our front lawn, lamentably unspoiled by feathered bodies. Out back, it is the same. I say "lamentably" because morbid as it sounds, I feel bereft without them. This strikes me as shameful, but I can't help the feeling; it breathes out of me, sighing against the glass. I finger the window's coolness and long to hold something supple. Even dead things can be surprisingly supple. A blur of color just outside makes me jump, a chirp of surprise escaping. Several feet away, Xavier waves and grins, his fog-dampened hair the deepest black and sticking to his forehead. I let him inside.

"What were you thinking just now?" he asks, laughing.

"Nothing much."

"You were thinking *something*. You didn't see me for a long time."

I get Xavier a beer and ask him to the gathering. A note of caution sounds somewhere in my head, says Itzel would object, but I hear myself extending the invitation anyway. Xavier observes me like he's my caretaker. I like having him around. It's hard to tell from his reaction if he means to come or not. Maybe he's mumbling, or maybe I'm not attending well. It seems to me we're both nervous, and I wish we still had the birds to mull over.

"You and Itzel doing okay?" He sits at the dining table slipping one flower after another into the vase Itzel set out.

"Yep," I say, admiring the way Xavier's nimble fingers grasp the stems and ruffle the heads. For many minutes he maneuvers the flowers, drawing his chin back into his neck to get the wider view, then once more leaning into his project. He looks as if he needs a shave. Sometimes he drinks the beer and chuckles at me, but mostly we're silent. When he's finished, the result is good enough that I carry the vase to the living room and position it right where Itzel told me to.

"Glad to hear it," he calls after me as if ten minutes had not intervened, as if that intervention of time had not charged the present moment beyond all reckoning. Soon I am in the bedroom, and I hear myself call to him. It almost sounds like beckoning, but that hardly seems possible. Winged panic flaps and careens inside me. Just like that, he stands in the doorway looking stiff and old and handsome in that Latin way I adore. Words. My next words mean everything.

"I need to show you something," I say.

From beneath the bed, I retrieve the plastic bag of crafting supplies and from among them the last of the new and improved coffins, this one yet unfinished, unneeded. Rows of brown chain and stem stitches embroider the sides, pale pink French knots, too. Gray feathers frame the top, and in the middle, a cross composed of intricate pink glass and copper beading. "The tips of the cross will be white," I explain. "I've got ceramic seed beads for that part." I hold out the coffin for Xavier to examine, but he won't take it from me.

"*This* is how you've been burying your birds?" he whispers. His long fingers graze the stitching, pause at the cross, caress my knuckles. We're so close I sense his warmth. I love Itzel, if only for the sake of how we used to be or how we might be again. I do not love Xavier, the man I've drawn into the bedroom Itzel and I share. I will never love Xavier. For this reason, I hold still, or more specifically, I manage to keep my head still, to concentrate on one slightly misshapen copper bead even as my body sways like it would tumble all the way down.

"It's beautiful," he says, and seems to mean it. Then he turns and walks away. By the time I get to the kitchen window, he is disappearing through the gate linking our backyards, his empty beer bottle smashed on the patio near Itzel's favorite chair.

⸙   ⸙   ⸙

The white seed beads turn out to be just what the last coffin needed. I had not intended to finish it—and definitely not today—but Xavier's departure hollowed out the house, left me stunned and drifting from room to room. I wish Itzel would come home. I wish I had more birds to bury, which is not the same as wishing more would die. It was a comfort to reach for the beads, their satisfying heft and delicious click irresistible.

Truly the coffin is coming to life now, full of contrast and balance. Itzel would have better language, but we stopped talking about art after I quit my classes. My hands work quickly, a meditation whose pattern loosens my breathing and siphons pressure from my head.

Only two beads to go when I hear Itzel's car in the driveway. "Shit!" I shove the lot under the bed, beads and feathers scattering amidst the dust. Rushing through the house, I check the time and discover I've been sewing for two hours. Felt like fifteen minutes. Broom in hand, I head out back to clean up the shards of Xavier's bottle but find instead a note taped to the chair. It says simply, *Lo siento—X.* The glass is gone. That things between Xavier and me should have come to this, to an actual expression of something I assumed would remain secret, harmless. What to make of him? What to make of me?

⬗   ⬗   ⬗

The pleasantries and laughter, the chewing and swallowing of expensive food, the spills and refills of trendy cocktails eventually yield to petty territorialities and tiffs over nothing that matters. By two hours in, the general zeal is overwhelming, but cheese to slice, crumbs to wipe, and napkins to replenish somewhat buffer me. Itzel is mad at me. The flowers, she said just before her guests arrived, are nicely arranged. "Inspired," she said. I confessed the credit belonged to Xavier, and her face slackened. She didn't ask why he was here or for how long, just went on readying our home in that icy way she summons when angry. I didn't even tell her I'd invited him to the party. Now I'm trying to make eye contact with her, exchange expressions that prove we're still in this together, but she won't budge.

When it happens, when the big thing happens, I am pretending to tidy one of the food tables so I won't have to talk to anyone. Occasionally one of them pauses in their rounds to gaze upon my face and declare me a dead ringer for Manuel's *Gypsy.* "Itzel's right!" they announce, but I'm not sure they believe it. Otherwise, I am left alone. Itzel stands across the room with her hip jutted. She's chastising a colleague for calling *La Gitana Tropical* the American *Mona Lisa.*

The man is about to retort when something slams into the picture window facing the backyard, the bang so loud the vibration registers in the roof of my mouth. A flurry of gray and yellow drops to the ground against the night's thickening canvas of fog. The room quiets. I hurry to the window and peer down at the little creature. Several guests do the same. A waxwing with its neck obviously broken quivers, then stops breathing. It is marvelous to see what a small bird has generated such a commotion. Waxwings don't normally fly by night, and I wonder if this, then, is the last of the boozy birds, the last one flushed out at closing time, cast into the gloom, too disoriented to find its way home.

"There's a still life on your patio, Itzel," the woman next to me calls over her shoulder. People laugh. Itzel glances our way but is whetting her indignation over the American *Mona Lisa* remark. It would take more than a dead bird to divert her.

What's clear to me is the bird cannot lie there in a crumple while Itzel's guests feast on canapés and old wine, pontificating until their eyes roll back. To get a better view, I edge to my left and lean forward until my nose touches the cold glass. The head is damp and bloodied but the rest still silky, still pretty. And it has come to me, this last bird. It has come to me to die, so I'll tender it to the grave as I did its peers. I cannot do otherwise.

Itzel doesn't appear to notice when I slip away, and the unbroken muffle of noise beyond the bedroom door confirms her party is fine without me. I affix the last two seed beads, my movements brisk as reflexes even as my hands sweat. Will she disdain me for this? Will it grow the still space between us? But I recall the bird outside on the wet cement and hurry my stitches. When finished, el ataúd es hermoso.

Wending my way through the guests, I tuck the coffin under my arm. I do not desire attention, especially not Itzel's, but neither do I wish to dishonor the thing I have created, the thing I am doing. She sees me right away, is watching me, and I wonder now if perhaps she has watched me all evening. In the kitchen, I get a pair of latex gloves then go to the back door and step into rain boots. She draws nearer, and though the gesture is nearly imperceptible, shakes her head at me. *No,* she is saying. *Stop.* I wipe my free hand on my pants, muster the small smile I reserve for Itzel, my mate, and let myself out.

Surprisingly cold, the moist air fills my body, almost like breathing pure oxygen. The guests watch through the window, but obliquely, as if they are not watching at all. Itzel isn't among them. Gingerly I lift the bird, careful to cradle its head and neck, and lay it in the coffin, its bed a square of velvet softened from beneath by a layer of cotton batting. Another square of velvet comes to shroud the body, makes a holy mystery of its silly death. The lid goes on last, its profusion of beads glistening in the light beaming from our little home.

Only when she speaks do I realize Itzel has followed me outside. "You need to come back in, Loma." This is what she says. Not, "What are you doing?" or "What is that?" Just

"Come back in." She glances up at her guests on the other side of the window and smiles sheepishly. Dumbly, one of them waves.

From the backyard's deeper darkness, Xavier's voice reaches us. "I heard it hit. I'll dig you a hole, Paloma. Give me a minute." Then he adds, "Pobrecito." He is only a silhouette, the dark shadow of a man closing a gate, taking up my shovel, but tension emanates from this shadow, and Itzel stiffens in reply. For several moments, she considers Xavier. Probably he's considering her too, but I can't see his face. Then she comes to me, stops just inches away and looks down at the box in my hands.

"Dio mio," she says. She smells like beer and cilantro.

"I have to," I whisper.

She touches the beads, traces the stitching, then my fingers, outlining them the way children do with crayons. "I see," she says, and turns to Xavier. When she reaches for the shovel, he pulls back, but she says, "Por favor," and he relents, tells her to follow him. Xavier then leads Itzel to my secret graveyard, the one she was never meant to see. There, the last of the poor, dead, drunk bird graves must be dug. Bearing the coffin, silently offering my customary prayer, I follow just behind them.

EMBER

CHUCHI MARVELS AT THE SPARKS, THE EMBERS BRIGHTEN-
ing this darkest night, and I guess they are kind of pretty. You
look up, eyes watering against the cold, and can't tell the sparks
from the stars. We don't have a tree this year, so maybe smol-
dering flakes of the Brownsburg Public Library are as close to
Christmas lights as we're gonna get. Chuchi tilts his head all
the way back, mouth open, and the orangey glow from the
library illuminates his features. Little swirls of dark hair cling
to his neck. He needs a shower.

They don't always burn them down. They razed the art
gallery and put in a Starbucks, leveled the museum too, not
that it was anything great. But every time we pass the muddy
cavity where it stood, I feel kind of empty. Chuchi's no good at
expressing his feelings, but I can tell it also bothers him. "Mad
world, mad kings," he said the first time he saw it. I wrote that
one down.

A few weeks ago it was the Santa Maria Art Academy. Sister Esperanza had been running that thing since Chuchi and
I were kids. Our mother even enrolled us one summer. Pick

up some culture, Ma said. I don't know about culture, but we learned how to tie-dye T-shirts on which Sister had written *Santa Maria Art Academy* in fabric marker. It fits him like a sausage casing, but Chuchi still wears his to bed. Sister had us painting trees and bowls of fruit and signing our names like we were real artists. We loved that part, would practice our signatures for ages before committing them to thick and curling watercolor paper. Sometimes she'd tell us to close our eyes and sense the beauty all around us. Those were her exact words. I know because I wrote them down. Chuchi said Sister Esperanza must have been a hippie in another life.

The Academy occupied a tiny house the parish had no use for. Sister painted it herself every few summers, so it was always bright white but leaned gently to the west and looked as if it housed as many squirrels as paintbrushes. Chuchi said the parish only let her have it that long because it was in our neighborhood . . . with all the Latinos. Anyway, it worked out fine for a while, but yeah, they burned it down, just like they're burning the library tonight.

On the Santa Maria's last day, a few of us gathered to watch the smoke billow. Neighbors mostly. Lorencito, who lives next door to Chuchi and me, wept to his mamá about a Popsicle-stick donkey he'd been working on and knew full well the flames had gobbled up. Sister Esperanza loved to have the kids make—from thousands of Popsicle sticks—decorations for Día de los Tres Reyes: the manger, the camels, the kings, a bunch of palm trees. Then she'd display them from just before Christmas through January 6. Mostly the kids who made them would drag their papás down there to have a look, but Chuchi and I always stopped in, too.

In its final moments, the Academy hissed and groaned until

nothing but a heap of coals remained. The mayor said go to the city website. There's an enhanced Q&A page that addresses potential questions and concerns. I pulled out my phone. The Q&A seemed pretty thorough. Then she said some stuff about progress and the technological age. Anthropocene, she called it. Chuchi said she used the word wrong, but I wouldn't know, so I wrote it down to look up later.

When it was time to go, Chuchi wiped his nose on his sleeve and said, "All ashes, but blow on a dead man's embers and a live flame will start." I still don't know what he meant by that. Chuchi's kind of a genius—the school explained this to our mother early on—but he'd forget to eat or brush his teeth if I didn't remind him. Though he's older than me by two years, he'll forever be my plus-one. Even if I get married and have children, Chuchi's with me for life. I've accepted that.

So tonight, December 21, the longest night of the year, they're burning the library, and that should be the last of it. Even people's little free libraries have been flattened. I'm pretty sure there's nothing left in Brownsburg for them to burn or raze, no more dead weight to jettison on our race to the electric future—Chuchi's words, not mine. But he said them sarcastically because he knows he's smart and assumes he's got one up on everyone. Which I kind of think he does.

Mrs. Norris—she's the librarian—hustled out clutching Mr. Whiskers right before they lit it up. She was breathing hard and crying, and Mr. Whiskers put all his claws out in that panicky way cats have. You could even see where Mrs. Norris was bleeding in places from Mr. Whiskers digging in.

Flames quivering behind her and firemen at the ready, the mayor repeated her words about progress and digital literacy, or sometimes she said digital readiness. We may be a small town, she said, but we don't have small ideas. Then she mentioned SpaceX and 5G and nanotechnology, and everyone nodded. I read over the Q&A again. It struck me, this time, as a little less thorough.

When the crowd begins to thin, I turn to Chuchi, who is still watching the sky, and ask if he's ready to go home. "O joy," he says, not even looking at me, "that in our embers is something that doth live." At this moment, this very moment, a vast V of geese honking praise for the moon and stars sails by overhead. Chuchi says, "See? See how the birds fly unaware in the hurt of the night?" And I don't know what he means, but I write down his words.

THIS NEW TURN

AT ITS CORE, THE STORY IS A SIMPLE ONE. FOR AGES humans gave birth to humans and animals to animals. Then one day a woman in La Crosse, Wisconsin, gave birth to a puppy, a Lab-greyhound mix, to be exact. It weighed a pound, they said, though I don't suppose that meant much to most of us at the time. It was well known that human newborns weigh around eight pounds, but average folks knew nothing of the birth weight of dogs. Later, after the story had broken and the puppy grew into a twenty-five-pound twelve-week-old, the woman consented to an interview.

Everyone watched. If you went for a coffee at the appointed hour that day, you'd have been forced to serve yourself. Sidewalks and streets emptied, sparrows and the ticking of crosswalk lights the only sounds. Counters and shops went untended in the midsummer heat. We found our seats, gripped our screens, quieted our breathing, and listened for the prognosis. We the patient. She the pathology we hoped wouldn't spread. Surely she'd explain how it happened, comfort us with certainty that the paradigm hadn't altered. We needed, in those early days, to believe her experience had been a fluke, a freak of nature. Maybe she'd taken some weird supplements or an experimental drug. Maybe she was a sexual deviant and had done something unspeakable. Maybe she'd been implanted by aliens. Somehow even that would have been a relief.

Instead she said she had no idea how it happened. She'd been plugging along leading a normal life: working, getting married, then trying to get pregnant once she and her husband managed to purchase a little home. She smiled almost demurely as she spoke, fingered a button on the cuff of her blouse. The new house—she reflected dreamily—had roses in the front yard. The only thing missing was a child. Here she turned big glassy eyes on her husband, and he squeezed her hand. We all shook our heads then, as if to say, *That poor woman.* But there was also a degree of consternation in our head shaking. Nothing she'd said so far offered any insight, gave us any hope or comfort. We had longed to draw a thick line between her and the rest of us. But her dark brown hair, her shiny pink lips, the roses, only made us squirm in our seats. She *was* us.

In response to the very worst of the interviewer's questions, the woman rolled her eyes and said, no, she had not had carnal knowledge of a beast, and no, her husband hadn't done that either. On the matter of her diet, she expressed a preference for grilled cheese on rye and tomato soup in the winter, hot dogs and cold watermelon in the summer. Cucumbers were among her favorite vegetables, and peaches her favorite fruit. There were chewable vitamin C pills during cold and flu season, and when the pollen was high, an occasional Benadryl. No other medications.

"So when did you realize something was wrong?" the

interviewer finally asked. We held our breath. Pupils dilated. Pores opened. Millions of bodies poised to receive even the faintest of clues. After a year of trying, she explained, all the usual signs and eventually a positive home test convinced her she was pregnant. She had even made an appointment with her gynecologist. But then, six weeks into the pregnancy and three days before her appointment, she went into labor. A few hours later, Bailey was born. The interviewer's eyebrows rose. Our eyebrows rose.

"Well, we had to give her a name," she explained, tucking a wave of hair behind her ear. "I mean of course we were shocked, but that wasn't her fault. We weren't about to reject her. She'll always be our girl." And that was the part of the interview the news shows got stuck on. Later. When they dissected every second of video for days and weeks after. *Our girl.*

Guest scientists suddenly intoned on neoteny, the condition whereby adult animals retain juvenile traits. "So humans have cultivated neotenic qualities in their animals since the Neolithic era," they explained, spectacles flashing. "One could certainly make the case that this trend has only strengthened in the last few decades, perhaps to a perilous degree . . ." And even though it seemed like the scientists had more to say, like essential caveats went unuttered, that was all the cable personalities needed to hear.

"Look. We've been treating our pets like children for some time now," the personalities said. Sweating. Flaring. "Calling them 'kids,' 'our boys and girls,' saying we love them, that they're as much a part of our families as our own children. *Our own children!* We feed them vitamins and wheat-free kibble. We stuff them into Halloween costumes, hold funerals for them, and bury them in cemeteries. We weep and take antidepressants when they die and write elegies that end with hopeful images of them in Heaven. *That's* what happened," the talking heads theorized, "we lost our sense of proportion. Neoteny on steroids. *We* did this."

For a while that struck most of us as mere hyperbole. We chuckled. You can't *make* something like this happen, no matter how you treat your pets. Absurd. We shook our heads and got on with life, chalked the whole thing up to nature's penchant for disturbing us from time to time. It's a natural check, we said. A way to keep us from getting too smug about our own understanding of the cosmos. Like UFOs and crop circles. Pandemics. Dark energy. A vocal minority even pronounced the story pure fiction, a grand scheme to distract us from government corruption, corporate tyranny, global warming. Just so much dog wagging (no pun intended, of course).

But then it happened again.

A cat this time, born to a thirty-eight-year-old woman in Boca Raton. Then another cat in Los Angeles. Then more dogs and cats and cats and dogs and more and more until fully 50 percent of all newborns were either canine or feline and the other 50 percent human. It was all anyone talked about. Breathless news cycles nearly imploded with the possibilities: the end of the world, a curse, a virus, neoteny again, recapitulation, a changeling epidemic, an animal revolution—payback for all those factory farms and puppy mills. Whatever the reason, the reality had to be dealt with, and at first many couples vowed childlessness. The number of vasectomies went up 12,000 percent. "We're not having *freak* babies!" they cried, the women especially, chins quivering and wet lashes blinking away sweet images of the lives they'd never have. No more toddling dimpled faces, tricycles, tutus. No more Little

League. Men cried, too. We all did. How could we help but mourn a way of life forever gone from us?

Soon, though, another feeling entered the mix. It started with the commercials. Surprisingly, the first one wasn't for dog or cat food but rather laundry detergent. It showed a woman walking down a sidewalk feeling goofily proud of her little girl's gleaming white eyelet dress. The girl bobbed along in front while the mom trailed behind pushing a stroller containing a lop-eared puppy in a pale blue shirt. When she passed the camera, the mom smiled, did a little eye roll, and said, "If only they *stayed* this clean!" And we all got the message. The "they" could only mean the *kids*, which could only mean the little girl in the white dress and the puppy in the stroller. And before we could even process our astonishment, more such commercials blossomed like spring flowers. We found ourselves amidst a whole field of them, their heady fragrance prevailing upon our senses like opium.

Add to the commercials a handful of celebrities saying positive things about the change, and it's no mystery how we came to revise our thinking. "You give love. You get love. That's family," a famous actress weighed in. A prominent tech mogul said he'd long viewed his dogs as his kids. "So what's the big f—ing deal?" The news shows beeped out the profanity, but you could tell what he'd said. He posed the question with a vigorous shrug, like a challenge to all the knuckleheads out there.

But it was a minor celebrity who made the biggest impact, an astrologer who'd gained fame in California for helping police find abducted children. She went on a show one day—her face pale, her long hair frizzing—and with a smooth voice, told of Xana from Asturian myth. Xana, a sometimes beneficent, sometimes dangerous spirit, replaced human babies with her own xaninos because she could produce no milk and needed someone to care for them. The astrologer paused, smiled serenely. "So you see, everybody. These ones are sweet too. You have only to love them." Even as we doubted her reasoning, we couldn't help but nod our agreement with her conclusion. We had only to love them.

Soon we were buying gifts for little bundles of feline and canine joy. We found ourselves asking, "Puppy, kitty, or baby?" like it was a thing we'd always done. And no matter the answer, the response was the same: "How *exciting*!" We threw showers with bone- or fish-shaped cakes and presents of dog beds and scratching posts (natural tree stumps with bark were in vogue). We played a shower game called Bow Wow or Meow Meow and laughed until our sides hurt. And after delivery, we festooned our cars with PROUD PAW PARENT bumper stickers. We posted pictures of ourselves with our new arrivals and entered friendly competitions to see which pair looked most alike. It was always a droopy-faced dad with a hound puppy or a blond-haired mom with a Himalayan kitten. At first-birthday parties, it became a trend to hold viewings of these kinds of pictures. We'd point and giggle and crack jokes at the bad ones, gasp and exclaim "Wow!" at the good ones. Some of the likenesses were stunning.

And if in the midst of such celebrations a smile sometimes wilted, a face grew ashen, eyes misty and haunted—seeing and not seeing—we looked away or suggested the refreshments table where we hoped sugar and salt might salve their anguish. Happily, that doesn't happen as much these days as it did then, during the transition. Today's youngest parents were actually born after the change, so they've never known otherwise, and many grew up with dog and cat siblings. Some even *prefer* to have puppies or kitties and are disappointed to learn they'll be having a baby. "Babies are so much more work," they explain. "You can litter train a kitten in no time. Babies wear diapers for *ages*. And *think* of all the complications. What if they're not happy? What do you do?" They shake their heads and look pensive, really considering the matter. "Dogs and cats give you unconditional love and ask so little in return. That's nice. You can live your life that way."

So it seems we've finally adjusted. What was once a staggering blow is now more or less normal. That isn't to say there aren't lingering problems. There are. Insurance coverage and inheritance laws have proven thorny. A political movement advocating the personhood of dogs and cats has gained momentum. Now that they're born to humans, they're legally recognized US citizens, so they must also be persons, or so the argument goes. Most people won't bend that far, however. Not yet anyway. "That's not the measure of a human," opponents say. "Humans have souls, know the difference between right and wrong, contemplate their own existence. Dogs and cats just lick their butts." That's what the detractors always come back to. Nothing dehumanizes like butt licking. And then there's the problem of class distinction. A certain hegemony has crept in, and you can tell many of the human-born animals feel superior to their less rarified peers. Entitled. But none of these problems has proven especially crippling, and all in all we seem to have adapted rather well.

Just the other day I was at a kitty shower, and for the first time in ages I saw that haunted expression creep into the features of one of the guests. Now that I think of it, it was the expectant father who looked that way. His wife, who didn't show at all, had been laughing along with the others at the Leash and Collar game when his smile froze, became almost grotesque as he strained: neck tightening, eyes glazing, brown cheeks draining to a greenish gray. What was he thinking? Who can say? Maybe he imagined showing the son he wasn't having how to dribble and shoulder feint and jump-cut. Maybe he visualized watching the next World Cup with a cat curled on his lap. Maybe an image of the whiskers and teeth and tail in his wife's womb had come to him unbidden, or still more striking, a vision of the birth itself. Would there be an umbilical cord to cut? *Could* he? And what of the amnion—the birth sac—through which he'd just be able to discern the wet and matted fur of his new offspring? Would his wife, like a mother cat, gnaw it away before suffocation extinguished their joy?

Perhaps in that moment, when smile dissolved into grimace, the hazy membrane clouding his vision had split, clawed apart by his need to understand how his life had come to this. What provokes an expression like that? What dark torment? Whatever it was, we filled his listing cup with punch and piled cake onto his plate and jostled his shoulder until he revived enough for the party to go on.

BLOODLETTING

IF ANTOINE HADN'T BEEN SUCH AN ASS, MARIA NEVER would have taken up with Pablo, and truth be told, Pablo was the real trouble now. The fur for one. Everywhere. Like pine needles. The messes for another: pointy tacks of litter under-foot, barfed-up things, sofa arms shredded by his shiny razor claws. But all that could be managed, even cheered for its reas-suring dullness. The problem haunting Maria now was del-icate. Violent. How to explain? Words died on the tongue, though *vampiric* (or was it *vampirish*?) came often to mind.

It began with Antoine. The handsomeness of him, that was Maria's upending. She'd had other boyfriends, but none so fetching, and always wondered if exceptional good looks might attenuate the burden imposed by a boyfriend's shortcomings. Because, after a while, boyfriends grew tiresome, and you found yourself hard pressed to justify their continued presence in your life. Maria had had so many disappointing boyfriends that she'd nearly denounced the whole class of them. In the end, she amended her decision to allow for one exception: if a gloriously handsome man came along and happened to find her as attractive as she found him, she'd give it another go. Anyway, who was she kidding? Boyfriends couldn't be sworn off. The world was built for twos.

Glistening curls, smooth olive skin, deep meaningful eyes— that was Antoine. Exception incarnate. She'd been unable to look away. Soon his things edged out hers in the apartment she alone had occupied for a placid if wistful year. His clothes colonized the front of the closet so that she had to reach into spidery corners for her own. His food sprawled across the top shelf of the refrigerator. His hair products claimed the bathroom, his shows the television. Incorrigible—that was the word that had come to her not two weeks after he moved in.

Worse yet, she always had to remind him to pay his half of rent and utilities. And though she did so as pleasantly as anyone could, Antoine usually responded with eye rolling and a sigh. He even took credit for things she did. Like when he'd been tapped to write his grandmother's eulogy and found he wasn't good with words, Maria stepped right in, wrote the whole thing while Antoine napped. Everyone intoned on the moving sentiments they supposed were Antoine's, but instead of shifting credit to Maria, he only thanked them and went for more crab dip. Never even mentioned her name.

He's a fixer-upper, Maria laughed to herself. Gently, she'd tried to correct some of his ways, but to no avail. He wouldn't be guided, not by her at least. So what became obvious in Antoine was a kind of ordinary, sickening greed.

But there were worse infractions, too. Private ones.

One night, a few months into their cohabitation, Maria washed their dinner dishes while Antoine watched Bundesliga and hollered at the television. She had shaken her head and smiled at his antics—more from habit than because they charmed her—then dried her hands and gone to the sofa to be near him. Absently, he wrapped an arm around her shoulders, and soon she fell asleep. When she awoke, the television was off, and Antoine had his hands up her shirt kneading her breasts, his mouth drifted open.

"Come on," he said, gesturing toward the bedroom, smiling like a man accustomed to abundance.

Maria sat up and deliberated. He had *such* a lovely face, but she was headachy and tired. "Nah." She smiled apologetically and ruffled his hair. "In the morning."

But he wheedled and cajoled and by degrees wore her down. It wasn't force. She'd consented in the end, but it certainly wasn't courtesy. He knew she didn't want to, that she'd only yielded for his sake. When he finished, he went to the kitchen and made a sandwich, asked, after he'd put away the bread and mustard, if she fancied one too. Then, without even brushing the crumbs from the counter, he crawled back into bed and turned out the light. Within minutes, he was snoring. Maria took several aspirin and considered whether she liked Antoine, whether she would be pleased if he died in his sleep.

Exceptional good looks, it turned out, didn't amount to much.

So when Maria opened the apartment door one day and found Pablo sitting there, when she brought him inside, gave him ham, brushed his matted fur with Antoine's comb, when she took him to the vet—that very afternoon—for shots and a once-over, when she brought him back home, opened a can of high-end cat food, put down a dish of water, and finally curled up with him on the sofa, she did so knowing perfectly well Antoine hated cats. *Hated* them. He hated their *aloof, imperious, indifferent secrecy*—his words when he found them napping together. Maria nearly told Antoine "aloof" and "indifferent" meant the same thing but thought better of it. Instead, she laughed lightly at his fury and made him dinner.

That was her custom—to spread sweetness across the rough shards of everything ugly—and Maria knew this about herself. Friends and family sometimes worried she was too passive, "too nice," but she felt no concern, figured it was in her DNA. Anyway, nothing to be gained by nastiness. Things had a way of working out if you only let them.

Whether Pablo constituted such a solution is a matter of some complexity. You could say the Antoine problem worked out as a result of Pablo's arrival. One too many times Antoine came home to Maria and Pablo in bed together: Maria sleeping peacefully, her long dark hair fanned out beside her, and Pablo flopped across Antoine's pillow like he was the boss of everything. The neat rows of useless pink nipples on Pablo's belly especially vexed Antoine. Too often he encountered cat vomit in his shoes or sheaths of claw snagged in his cashmere sweaters.

And though he was loath to admit it, even to himself, Antoine found Pablo unnerving. Except for white patches on his belly and feet, Pablo's fur was deepest black, and at night his sleek form merged with the gloom. When Antoine roused for a drink of water or to use the bathroom, he never could tell where Pablo lurked until his luminous eyes blinked open to watch Antoine pass. Like torches. Like warning beacons. Like something unspeakable. Who would bring such a thing into a house? As if it were a little person. What did it even contribute? How did Maria know it wouldn't turn on them?

Antoine brought Maria flowers and candy. He taxed his brain for less obvious bribes, but who knew what women wanted? He massaged her feet. Once. He wiped away his crumbs when he finished eating. He thought himself a very good boy. But every time he pressed his perfect lips to Maria's ear and whispered, "Baby, come *on*, be nice to me. We can find him a new home," every time he ran his fingers up her arm and kissed her neck, the ever-sanguine Maria laughed and shook her head. Antoine tried the opposite tactic, too: yelling and stomping around, rumpling his hair, threatening to leave, but the result was the same. So finally, he packed his things.

Pablo watched him fill cardboard boxes that smelled of oat-meal, watched as he made neat towers of expensive shirts and silk boxers. And when Antoine tried shooing him away, Pablo laid his ears flat and hissed, his cavernous mouth all pearly fangs and red soft tissue. He would not budge from his gar-goyle perch on the dresser. And because this position put Pablo at eye level with Antoine, Antoine did his best to pretend Pablo wasn't there and hurried his packing, finally abandoning tidy towers for hasty piles and a quick exit.

The Antoine problem had worked out.

The Pablo problem was just getting going.

The funny thing is, right at first, you couldn't have con-vinced Maria Pablo was anything but a milagro straight from the heavens. *Glorious*, she whispered winter afternoons when the living room filled with sunshine and the contented rumble of Pablo's purr. How lovely to feel full and warm and genial in this way. Maybe she was a stereotype now: a single woman with a cat. Let the jokes commence. But there was something so tranquil about her life with Pablo, so uncomplicated. She had not known she needed him, but she did.

Over time, she learned what he liked and took genuine pleasure both in having someone to please and in pleasing him. It felt nice to stop off on her way home from work and order takeout for two, to say, "He'll have the fish," and see the cashier nod. And then at home, Pablo's nose would pulse excitedly at the savory aroma, his tail stiff and tall. He'd rub his cheek round and round Maria's ankles. And if he'd done some mischief while she was away—hacked up a slimy cigar of matted fur, broken her favorite vase, shredded a bit of the new ottoman—well, he could hardly be blamed. Pablo was a creature guided entirely by instinct. He had no choice in how he behaved, and this made all the difference to Maria. With no bad feeling whatsoever, she cleaned up the slime, glued the vase, tossed a throw over the ottoman, and beckoned Pablo to her. She loved to stroke the top of his head, his little skull so solid just there and his flimsy ears like darkest velvet between index finger and thumb.

♦ ♦ ♦

The first time Pablo bit her, Maria yelped but laughed too. "For goodness' sake!" she said. "Why'd you do that?"

Pablo peered up at her, right into her eyes, gold ringing his enormous pupils like two solar eclipses. An admonishment seemed in order, so Maria wagged her finger and called him a bad kitty. But even as she applied iodine to the punctures his teeth had left in her wrist, she felt no anger toward him, merely a desire to coax out his better instincts, to train him as all pets could and should be trained.

The biting, however, continued. Little nips that obeyed no discernible pattern: sometimes as Maria fondled Pablo's hot ears, sometimes when she set down his food. Sometimes he latched onto her ankle while she stood in the kitchen preparing dinner. And all her tactics for training him failed. She fussed at him, said "No!" as loudly and firmly as she could muster. She clapped her hands, even (reluctantly) misted him with water, but he only lowered his tail and sulked away. Soggy, insulted, yet unreformed.

A breakthrough of sorts came after Pablo inflicted an especially deep wound one evening, a wound that throbbed and reddened all the next day until Maria nearly visited the doctor. "You little beast!" she'd said, scratching Pablo's neck affectionately. "And what," she singsonged, "'hath charms to soothe a savage beast?' . . . or is it 'breast'?" Maria shrugged. Well, she'd heard somewhere that music calmed anxious animals, and what if Pablo was only nervous? Maybe he didn't like being left alone. Maybe secret feline afflictions stirred him, compelled him to lash out in this way.

After some trial and error, she found several artists Pablo liked . . . *more* than liked. Every time Maria played k.d. lang, Johnny Mathis, Doris Day, or Eydie Gormé, Pablo calmed visibly. His pupils shrank. His tail stopped whipping. His ears pivoted forward, and eventually he closed his eyes and fell asleep. His favorite song was Eydie Gormé's "Mala Noche." The soft, steady bongos and Eydie's creamy voice singing, "En las horas de mi insomnio fatal," made Pablo roll onto his back, put all four feet in the air, and snore. Maria thought it the cutest thing in the world.

Each day before work, Maria turned on the music, and when she came home, Pablo roused as if from an opium stupor, greeted her groggily, and began bathing his paws and belly. No more nipping, no more iodine. She giggled at him, called him her "little enigma," and sighed relief that her troubles were over.

Maria paused before the hall mirror to check her teeth for poppy seeds. She should have brushed again after the bagel, but she'd felt listless all morning and would be late for work as it was. The strange marks caught her eye right away. On her neck, several inches below her ear, a pair of puncture wounds. Gentle prodding found them sensitive. In all the times Pablo had bitten her, only her hands or wrists, feet or ankles had been involved, never her neck, and never while she slept. Maria shook her head and tensed the corners of her mouth. She turned to observe Pablo on the sofa. Absorbed in cleaning the tip of his tail, he wrinkled his nose and made a slurping sound.

"What did you *do*?" she said. He looked up. "You naughty thing!" Maria walked over and tickled his chin. Pablo closed his eyes and leaned heavily on her hand. He purred. With her other hand, Maria palpated the tender spots on her neck. They were curious, yes, even mildly concerning, but little more. What if Pablo *was* responsible? He was only a cat—an animal. Maria could never be angry at an animal.

In four weeks' time, Maria counted four sets of punctures on her neck, one per week. And she noticed that after a new wound appeared, she felt weak and woozy for days. Her body ran cold, and she kept envisioning her insides as a hollow cave, something drained and echoing. Fragments of barely recollected dreams came to her over lunch and in the bathroom— amorphous shapes that flamed and crept, dark vapors that girdled her throat until she gasped, and all the while, in the background, Eydie singing, "He's too close, too close for comfort, please not again."

Pablo, meanwhile, had never looked better. A solid layer

of muscle rippled beneath his gleaming fur as he negotiated the apartment, especially when he jumped. What a gorgeous, confident shape he made when he leapt through the air. Maria lifted her eyebrows every time. Visitors remarked as often on Pablo's beauty as on Maria's wanness. She laughed off their solicitude, agreed that she needed some sunlight and fresh air, but privately began to worry.

At night she battled drowsiness in hopes of catching Pablo in the act, but every time she checked, he was sleeping peacefully beside her. She considered shutting him out of the bedroom. That seemed logical. But the one time she tried, Pablo sat in the hall gaping up at her with such mournful eyes that she nearly wept on the spot. "Come on," she said, voice full of remorse, and he tootled into the room as innocently as a butterfly might approach its favorite flower. There would be no closed doors between Maria and Pablo.

Still, she did look pallid. That was inescapable. And it took more than a dozen high-necked blouses to conceal the wounds in their various stages of healing. One delirious night, she even thought of Antoine, tried to recall how it had been with him, with the other boyfriends, too, if it had been like this. She could recall injuries and suppressed worries, not unlike now, but by the end of those relationships, she had felt such *aversion*. Naturally she had smiled through it, but the awful feeling persisted, like nausea. For all her current troubles, she felt no aversion toward Pablo. Quite the opposite.

So Maria began searching in books and online. Were there others in her situation? If so, how had they coped? What did the experts say? She envisioned smiling veterinarians and animal psychologists, their keen tips listed alongside images of them cuddling their favorite cases.

Instead, she found a thing she had not expected but immediately understood she needed: a support group.

⸙   ⸙   ⸙

"I'm Megan, and I've successfully cohabitated with Sunny for two and a half years now." Megan smiled and held up a picture of an immense ginger tabby. He lolled on a flowered sofa, eyes slitted and staring into the camera, paws serenely padding the air. "He's a bit of a fatty, I'm afraid." Megan giggled. "He *loves* vanilla pudding. I know I shouldn't let him eat it, but who could resist that face?"

The circle of turtlenecked women laughed and nodded their assent. Maria laughed, too. The public library's meeting room had seemed toasty when she hurried in from the March wind, but the metal folding chair felt cold now. Maria kept shifting her weight from side to side.

"My name is Brady. Most of you already know Charles." She held up her phone, and a fluffy gray cat in a purple collar stared back at them. "We're going on eight successful months."

One by one, they introduced themselves and their cats. When it was Maria's turn, she waved shyly. "I'm Maria." Her voice echoed in the bare room. "And this is Pablo." She'd had trouble deciding which picture to share, finally settling on one of him in the sunshine, curled like a sweet roll and sleeping. "This is my first time, so I don't have any successes to report, but hopefully that's about to change."

In unison the women nodded and said "Oh yes" and "Absolutely!" It *would* change. She'd come to the right place, they said. Soon she'd understand how, in Brady's words, "strangely satisfying" this kind of relationship could be. She could, in fact, thrive in it. They chatted excitedly and plied Maria with ginger cookies, beef jerky, and hot cider. Stories, too. All of them like her own: the failed boyfriends, the cat's arrival, the bliss, then the punctures, the weakness, the mysterious creature who shared her life now.

As the newest of their assembly, Maria was treated like a favored pupil, her every query met with earnest concern. She scribbled down the details: wound care and camouflage; how to explain her lifestyle choice to family, friends, and coworkers; and especially how to combat anemia. Going forward, she'd have to cook on an iron skillet and eat more red meat. Black-strap molasses worked wonders if your stomach could take it. And Pablo, it turned out, could be trained to bite her just once or twice a month rather than weekly. That was a relief.

Only two questions remained. Amidst the consoling chime of dishes and chatter, Maria turned to Megan, whose large eyes made her look like a young girl. "Are we the only ones?" She whispered the words and rushed a cup of steaming cider to her lips.

"Let's see." Megan nodded. "I think we're missing Ashti this week, but otherwise, yeah, we're it."

Maria swallowed. "I mean are we the only group like this? The only women in this *situation*?"

"The only women to . . . Of course not! There are *tons* of these groups." The others—who'd coalesced around Megan and Maria, their floral warmth radiating—murmured their affirmation.

"It's just that, before all this, I'd never heard of such a thing," Maria said.

"No one talks about it," said Brady, "not out there at least." She gestured toward the world beyond the gray light of the library window. It was beginning to snow, and the women watched the pattern of it, their chests rising and falling.

"Are you all content with your decision to live this way? No regrets?" Neither blame nor acrimony dwelled in Maria's heart, especially where Pablo was concerned—he was only a cat—but she had to know.

The response was unequivocal. The boons—companionship, humor, tranquillity, respect—exceeded the bothers by the widest of margins, the women said. "They take something from us," Megan admitted, "but give-and-take's part of any relationship. It's not like they mean harm."

Maria fingered a cookie. A wave of heat reddened her cheeks, and her eyes watered. Someone proffered a box of tissues. "That's just how I see it," she said. "They're so innocent."

Megan bit into a strip of beef jerky and spoke with her mouth full. "At this point, I don't even mind sharing my blood with Sunny. *Really*. This is the happiest I've ever been."

Maria considered Antoine—his rapacity—and felt certain the women were right. How could a future with Pablo not be better than that? Especially now, with so much solicitude to fortify her, she felt hopeful. Things would work out. They always did.

⸭   ⸭   ⸭

On the stove, a heavy iron skillet—still steaming and coated in melted butter and bread crumbs from a corned beef sandwich. On the sofa, Maria—a velvet scarf around her neck, shiny lips moving up and down as she chewed and swallowed. On the coffee table, a hot mug of milk and molasses. She'd found her

stomach could manage the irony black syrup if she cut it gen-
erously with dairy fat. And on Maria's lap, Pablo—indolent,
seraphic, one radiant paw kneading the softness of Maria's
belly. Tenderly and only a little pale, Maria watched him into
the night.

CHICORY

EVEN NOW, I LIKE TO THINK OF MYSELF AS RATIONAL, inured to my father's oddball collection of superstitions and folksy ideas. I know crows don't attract lightning, and I almost never toss salt over my shoulder. Still. Here I am. At noon. On St. James' Day. In an overgrown Missouri field near the apartment I share with my father, I am chest deep in chicory and keeping as silent as if my life depended upon it. Because supposedly it does. Specifically, I am sawing at the hairy stems I've gathered in my left hand. Delicate blue chicory flowers shake their little heads at me while I work. In my right hand, a gold-plated letter opener, dull, but it's the gold that matters.

I set the bruised stems aside, shoulder sweat from my face, and reach for several more, careful not to grunt or breathe audibly. Papi's book was clear on this point. Make a sound of any kind during the gathering, and sure as sunset death will follow. When my father read this part aloud, I guffawed, but he only widened his eyes and wagged a finger. "No, mi'ja. Take it seriously." So I am trying to take it seriously, just in case.

Muscles burn as I bend over my task, and something about my pants, the way the knees have bagged out, makes me feel dumpy. I am already ludicrous, but ugly's worse. I should know better than this. I should move away, start my own life, but Papi takes such pleasure in any sort of conundrum requiring his unique brand of farm filósofo wisdom. At such moments, a rare tide moves him, and he rushes around the apartment like when my mother was alive. It's nice to see him happy.

The conundrum at hand involves, of all things, a trunk. Last month from Tía Estrella's estate came this old wooden affair with a big brass lock and no key. The only thing Papi recalls about Tía Estrella is that she liked poetry, but that doesn't explain the trunk. He prattles on and on about what could be inside and how to get it open without wrecking it. Wrecking a lock is bad luck, he says. Anything gained that way will curse you. As for calling a locksmith, my family has never liked strangers knowing its business. If we can do the thing ourselves, we will. And if we can't, we'll keep trying until we've made a definite hash.

Papi found the "solution" in one of his dog-eared books on folk remedies. It turns out chicory—cut with a gold blade on St. James' Day—magically opens even the most fortified of locked things. Hence my current situation.

Coming out of the weeds, I see her. Of course I do. Our new neighbor one apartment over, out for a walk. Supple vines of honey blond hair curl around her shoulders, and with each step, her sandaled toes grip as if they would root down into the earth. She is something like a Norse goddess. Recognition makes her pause and smile, but she's taking it all in: the fist of chicory, the knife, the sweat and filth besmearing my face and clothing. At best, I am a B-movie monster. All I can do is swear silently and hope she doesn't want to talk, which is ironic because any other day I'd jump at the chance. She's about my age and looks as if she'd smell of soap. Secretly I've hoped we might become friends. After high school, everyone I knew slipped off to college or piled into hipster apartments far away. Papi's and my apartment is decidedly non-hipster, but our still living together isn't weird. It's not "A Rose for Emily." It's just a thing that happened.

I smile and walk faster, practically running. I even point at my wrist, meaning my watch, meaning I'm late, only I don't own a watch. Must be a gesture I picked up from Papi. She probably thinks I stashed a body in the overgrowth. Confusion—maybe repulsion—registers, but she's polite. She nods and glides away.

Perfect.

I have no idea how long I'm supposed to remain silent, so I slip home, reticent as a cat. When Papi opens the door (he's been watching for me through the curtains), even his hushed voice startles.

"You got it?" But he's looking right at the sheaf of chicory in my arms, and I'm annoyed about seeing our neighbor, so I don't answer. "No problems?" He pats my cheek.

I shake my head and whisper, "Are you sure we can talk now?"

"Yeah, yeah. It's safe. Already one o'clock. Good job, mi'ja."

He's pleased. I can tell by the way he keeps blinking. While I soap my arms in the kitchen sink, he floats a blanket of paper towels across the dining table and rests the chicory upon it. Then he bends down and inhales, eyes closed, mouth curving into a goofy grin. "Mi'ja." He waves me over. "*Smell*. What does it remind you of?"

Mostly I smell dirt and summer, but there is something more. "Oregano?"

"Sí, y también?"

I shrug.

"Mamá's perfume. Don't you think?"

I inhale again, dipping lower this time. I do not smell my mother's perfume, but I nod and smile and say yes, *yes* until my father laughs and wipes his eyes.

"A good sign," he says.

✸   ✸   ✸

The candle is an odd touch. I can't decide if it's hokey or spooky and finally settle on mortifying. I keep seeing us— Papi and me—from our neighbor's perspective: the stacks of weirdo books, our brown eyes gone black in the dim room, Papi's dark magician hands, the smell of sofrito clinging to everything. What would a girl like that—pink cheeked with pale gold skin and rainwater hair—say to all this?

I hoist the trunk onto a towel and drag it across the floor to the dining room. "Mi'ja! Mi'ja!" Papi rushes over. "Don't do that! Let me help you. It's *heavy!*"

I wave him off. "I've got it."

"Mi'ja, I *saw* you straining." He's pushing like Sisyphus, overshoots the mark, then scoots the trunk back and back until the guttering candle lights it up. In the background, the TV has *Perry Mason*, one of his favorite shows, but the sound is down. On the witness stand, a woman's lipstick mouth dissolves into silent weeping while Perry's doleful eyes reproach.

Papi takes a deep breath, looks at me, and says, "Okay." It's all pretty dramatic, and I'm experiencing the effect of this even as I fortify part of my brain against him. My father can be very beguiling. I don't want to get too drawn into his bizarre world. I feel weird enough as it is, without the chicory: Cuban in a town with no other Cubans, gangly, smart, hairy, and definitely socially awkward. If I were prettier, I could be in one of those movies with the beautiful freaks who turn out to be superheroes. I'm too old for all that anyway.

The bundle of chicory, flaccid and browning, hardly impresses as a mythic force, so I ask if we should hang it upside down to dry for a few days before trying it on the lock.

"What?" Papi looks stricken. "No, no. Of course not! It doesn't matter how it looks."

Reverently he lifts a stem from the table and kneels down in front of the trunk. Tiny knots of faded blue fleck the foliage. From where I'm standing, Papi looks like he's praying. Maybe he is. He fusses with the leaves, then holds the chicory right up to the lock and waits.

Need I say nothing happens?

His shoulders do a little bounce, and he tries again, closer this time. Still nothing.

"Maybe it needs to touch the lock," I offer.

He tries this, tenderly pressing a bloom against the lock and pulling at the lid. The candle crackles. Anyone else might be cursing by now, but not my father. He looks up philosophically, smiles, and says, "Not today, mi'ja. Maybe not ever. We'll see."

And this is how my father routinely surprises me. Cutting through all his wacky ideas—these bright beams of reason. He is capable of such equanimity. No whining. No railing against matters beyond his control. Only one exception comes to mind: my mother's death.

Papi cooks rice and eggs for breakfast, and all the air is redolent of butter and garlic. The lush aroma makes me envision lounging in the sunshine admiring the smooth brown of my skin. Maybe the neighbor is there too, sleepy in the bright day. Maybe we're laughing.

This being the first Saturday I haven't had to work this month, I should go out. Make a friend. I've been around my father so much I'm starting to act old. I even carry my plate to the living room to watch *Perry Mason*. It comes on twice a day. Papi watches both times. Raymond Burr was gay, but my father doesn't know that, and I think it might somewhat dampen his enjoyment of the show if I mention it, so I don't.

From a taut line strung between kitchen cabinets, the chicory hangs. Waits. The day after our failure with the lock, Papi came into my room looking pensive and said, "Maybe you were right. It did seem sort of impotent." He whispered the word "impotent" and half covered his mouth as if the chicory might take offense. "We let it dry out, then try again."

It's been on the line ever since, a whole row of it by solemn degrees commending its juices to the thieving air. Honestly? You can tell it's ready, but Papi seems afraid to look at it, let alone touch it, almost like he's respecting its privacy. It vibrates with each little disturbance of the atmosphere, and it's obvious how stiff it's become. I'm not raising the issue, though. Papi's all tied up in little strings of hope about it. Why rush to an inevitable end?

"Going down to the market, mi'ja, get some chicken." Papi tugs at the waistband of his pants. His clothes look too big, and he needs a better haircut. My mother would be furious at the way clumsy shearing has flattened his natural curl. "I make something special tonight. Then let's try it, okay?" He glances at the chicory and nods in deference to its temperamental power. If he wore a hat, he'd tip it politely: *Good day, Master Chicory!*

After he's gone, I think my usual thought: what it would be like to have an apartment to myself. Papi's not dead in this scenario. We just don't live together anymore. And the vision is both scary and thrilling. In a silly moment, I spin around and dance my hands through the air only to find I've knocked one of the chicory branches off the line. But when I bend down and grasp the desiccated twig, a wave of dizziness stirs my head, and my legs liquefy. I stumble toward the kitchen counter and flatten my cheek against the cool surface, my heaving breaths loud in the silence. When the dizziness passes, I open my eyes, and there in front of me is our toaster. Something about it strikes me as odd, and at first I can't work out what it is.

Then I see it. Or rather, I don't. Where I should be reflected in the chrome, there is nothing, only a swirl of refrigerator and wood cabinets behind me.

I do not see my shirt.

My hair.

My face.

I draw the toaster to the edge of the counter and wave my hand before it, but there is only dead air. No me.

The bathroom mirror is the same. There is the wall behind me, there, my blue towel, but I'm nowhere to be found. I rap the glass and hear my knuckles knocking. I look down and see my arms, just like always. Hips and feet too. "What *is* this?" I try my voice, and though it comes out small, I do hear it. My first thought is I'm dead, that I've died and become a ghost. My second is I'm a vampire. These are not rational thoughts.

I set the chicory twig on the bathroom counter and clamber in close to the mirror. Just like that, I'm back. Huge brown eyes startle me so badly I duck away as if avoiding a punch, but then I'm laughing and crying, relief flooding through me. I turn to the chicory. Couldn't be a coincidence. Before I can chicken out, I pick it up again and disappear. Then I set it down and become visible once more. Several repetitions later, I'm so dizzy I have to lie down on the living room sofa.

The room tilt-a-whirls, and I close my eyes, swallow to keep my stomach down, grip the sofa so I don't slide off. Soon, familiar images march out of the darkness: tiny fairies with glass wings, talking eagles, trees cursed by witches, shadowy things that creep amidst the sugarcane—all the Cuba stories Papi told me when I was a child. And recent ones: the government plots to kill off Cubans with poisoned guava paste, or to kill off the poor with tainted vaccinations, or to kill off the elderly by paying Communist doctors under the table. I've long rolled my eyes at such nonsense. Even as a kid listening with nervous wonder, I'd draw the line when Papi insisted on the stories' veracity. I knew better. Or thought I did.

Now I meet a truth as inexorable as death: the white stucco ceiling, the Rika crackers, the refrigerator's labored hum, the bee outside tapping at the hot window, these all belong to Papi. The laws that bind them, that bind everything, belong to him. So, too, the crispy wand of vegetation on the coffee table. And me. I am merely a resident of my father's unaccountable cosmos.

Papi will be home soon, so I rouse myself from the sofa and rifle through his books, alert to any mention of chicory.

There's agreement on the plant's power to open locks, but only one book, in a dense and rambling footnote, mentions invisibility. I can't decide if finding it in print makes me feel better or worse. If Papi had known this, he would have said so. He'd be over the moon at such news, and ordinarily I would love to give him that gift, but I already know I won't tell him. When I hear his keys at the door, I slip the book back into place, hurry to the kitchen, and open the refrigerator.

"Hi, mi'ja," Papi singsongs, setting a bag on the counter, then pauses. "What's wrong? What's happened? You look funny."

"I'm fine," I say, and pour myself a glass of cold water.

◈   ◈   ◈

All through dinner Papi watches me, asks if I'm okay. Do I feel sick? Depressed? I try to reassure, but I'm nervous about him trying the lock again with the chicory. It's disgraceful, but I wish the secret of its power could remain mine, and for a reason I'd rather not own.

When the candle is lit and the television silently flickers *Kung Fu*, Papi lifts a chicory twig from the line and disappears. It is an extraordinary thing to witness, phenomenal, but also—I sense this—ephemeral, the result of forces so precariously aligned they cannot help but finally break apart. I used to have this dream I could fly the way you swim, by laboriously pumping arms and legs, but the moment my faith in the process wavered, I'd plummet to the earth. The chicory seems like that to me. One wrong move, and it all collapses.

I can only assume Papi still sees himself just as I did and doesn't realize he's invisible. The opportunity for me to gasp and feign all kinds of shock passes quickly, and I find myself guilty of the oddest deceit.

"I feel swimmy," he says. "Maybe I ate too much."

"It was so good," I say, which is true, though I hardly tasted my food.

"Mi'ja, what is it? Do I have something on my face?"

"No." I force a laugh. "Why?"

"You keep looking at my nose."

"Do I?" I sound weird, and I'm having a hell of a time calculating the distance from Papi's voice to his eyes, so I rub my forehead, the heels of my hands obscuring my vision, and claim a mild headache. "Go ahead," I mumble. "Let's see if this works."

Not three seconds pass before the lock clicks and the lid lifts about an inch. The chicory has indeed grown potent. Papi gasps. I can't see his face, but I know its expression—the big-eyed wonder, that bit of something held back in case all goes to ruin, one of the lessons disappointment teaches.

"Mi'ja!" he whispers. "Can you believe it?" Then there he is, crouching before the chest, both hands on the lid and the chicory lying on the floor beside him. He looks up at me, his eyes shining in the low light.

"No. I can't." It's no lie. I shake my head and laugh. "This is crazy." And I mean it.

Papi smiles. "No. It's not crazy at all. The book said so. Remember? Ready to see what's in here?"

I nod.

Warily—like any kind of terror could spring out—Papi lifts the lid until the chest's wide jaw yawns before us. Except for a single scrap of paper, the compartment is empty. No gold coins. No skull. No magic lamp. But for Papi the paper seems to have presence enough. Without even reaching for it, he takes a step back.

"Aren't you going to read it?"

"No! Not tonight." He's practically panting and pushes a black wave of hair from his forehead. "That's enough," he says. "Let's leave it for a day or two. Notes from the dead . . . I don't know, mi'ja." He bends forward, stretches two fingers toward the lid, like it has cooties, and closes it without a sound. In the kitchen he says something about dessert, then points at the chicory still on the floor, asks me to return it to the line. Panic twitches through me, but I think fast and tell him I'm going to lie down for a bit, that the headache is worse and I'm sleepy. This will definitely quiet him, because there is no malady in the world Papi thinks a nap won't cure.

"Okay." He nods. "I bring you some tea and those ginger galletas I made. Poor mi'ja." My father clicks his tongue and whispers about the kitchen on soft apothecary feet. Amidst his busyness, he eyes the trunk.

⸭ ⸭ ⸭

In the dark, I rest my hand on the hot plane of my stomach and see myself in the future. The scene is familiar. Decades from now, I'm being interviewed: "You still live with your father, right?"

I nod.

"Why . . . how, after all these years?" The voice is incredulous, accusatory. I squirm in my seat, squint into the lights. "Fear?" The voice prods. And yes, maybe fear played a role. Maybe fear and time were twin snakes unfurling. Maybe I chose safety.

"I guess I kept *meaning* to get out," I say, "but it was always easier to stay home and watch some shows with my father, pop some popcorn." I can't hear them, but out there somewhere millions of people gasp. *Pathetic*, they think. *What a wasted life*, they think.

Often, I think so, too.

◈   ◈   ◈

It's more dramatic and less shameful to say the idea came to me in the middle of the night, that I threw off the covers, sat up, and there it was: this *impulse*. But that's not the case. The truth is, the gist of the plan kindled when I read the footnote in Papi's book. Maybe I'm late admitting it, but that's definitely when. All day the idea trembled in the back of my brain, and now, at one in the morning, I'm ready to act. And I can't deliberate or self-loathing will overthrow all. I don't believe I'm a disgusting person, but there is no defending what I'm about to do.

Papi is a light sleeper, so I move silently through my room, into the hall, across the kitchen linoleum, and breathe more easily when I am again clutching the chicory and properly invisible. I check the toaster just to make sure. No dizziness this time. Maybe that's a good sign.

The hallway in our apartment building always smells of onion and cardboard. The onion is probably our doing, and I wonder if the neighbors despise us for it. Nearly as familiar to me as my own, her door comes into view. She has tied a blue ribbon around the knocker. I think, not for the first time, that only a sweet, friendly girl would do this. Ever since she moved in, I've entertained silly fantasies about my neighbor. We'd discover we both loved fried plantain and pickleball. We'd joke about being the only young people at the court. My dad would adore her, and she'd find him charmingly eccentric. Once or twice a week she'd come over for dinner and rave about his roast pork in mojo. She would not be vegan.

Beneath the door a sliver of light tells me she is either awake or asleep with the light on. I'm glad of this because I want to *see* her. That's the point. Stumbling around her apartment in the dark won't do me any good. I'm only going to stay for a minute. *Honestly.* That's all I need—to be in the company of someone my own age, to see how she decorates her living room, how she sits and stands, how she turns the blinds, makes a cup of tea, eats pretzels, lotions her elbows.

When the lock clinks open, I worry someone will have heard, but her living room is empty and the apartment carpeted in thick, sound-muffling shag. On the refrigerator, a birthday card. Her name is Astrid. I don't know why, but I'd expected it to be Megan or Hannah. Astrid seems almost exotic. A small shelf holds a stack of white coffee cups and a jar of Leroux instant chicory beverage. My finger grazes the label. What are the odds? Is it un pájaro de mal agüero? Papi would know if the omen is good or bad. From the kitchen I can see down the hall that a light is on in one of the bedrooms, and when the refrigerator quiets, a tiny clicking sound issues, irregular and metallic, then a sigh.

I won't belabor the way I feel at this moment—the pounding in my ears, the strangled breathing, the nausea threatening to upend Papi's ginger cookies. This is wrecking me. I'm going to hate myself afterwards, maybe forever.

Astrid sits on the edge of her bed clipping her toenails. Her belly pleats neatly along three lines, and long hair screens her face as she hunches over her feet. She doesn't even look up when I peek in. It had not occurred to me that she might be naked, and she isn't. There is a bra. Underwear, too. But I wish she were fully clothed. I just wanted to observe her watching a show or eating a peanut butter sandwich. Nothing private. There is a line to be observed, even here.

I feel my body move more fully into the room, occupying first the doorway, then an open area mere feet from her bed. When she picks up a file and begins smoothing her thumbnail, I notice how long her fingers are. Everything they do looks pretty. But with her face lifted, it's apparent she's been crying. Puffy pink skin rings her eyes, and her cheeks are splotchy. When her phone lights up, she slips off her bra, pulls her long hair forward over her shoulders, and smiles sweetly. She holds her phone out in front of her. "I'm waiting," she says, and lowers it so whoever it is can see her pale nipples push through a tangled haze of hair. I cover my eyes and with my other hand reach out toward a dresser, gripping the corner for balance, my head a whoosh of shame.

I should leave.

The voice on the phone is deep and male. I'm not sure it's speaking English. Astrid stands up and begins crying again. She stomps her foot and says something in a language that sounds Scandinavian. Over and over she does this, and every time she stomps, her breasts shake and she cries harder. An impulse to hug her, to mantle her nakedness, quickens my breathing even as I stand fixed and trembling. Finally she is yelling and crying all at once. Her free hand gestures and wipes, and soon tangles of hair bind to wet knuckles. Long strands come loose. But she only grabs more and more, pulls and pulls until silky threads encircle her fist like cotton candy.

Her words are inscrutable, but I recognize the heaving sound she makes between sobs, the tilt of shoulders and pelvis. She's *begging*. This tall, muscled girl who looks as if she could Viking her way through anything is pleading like a child. And in the background, behind Astrid, framed family photographs and gold-embossed books burden pale wood shelves. On the bed, a clutch of floppy stuffed animals huddles near the pillow.

When she finally launches her phone against the wall and sinks to her knees, I rush out of the room, out of Astrid's apartment, out of the building. In the courtyard, I throw up in a laurel bush. The wide night sky, its blue-black beset by stars, reproaches me. All that clear beauty gazing down upon my secret corruption. I am laid bare, and all I can do is throw up a second time, wipe my mouth on my shirt, and lie down in the grass. At this silent hour, solitude settles like dew. Soon I am cold and drenched.

⬧   ⬧   ⬧

It's nearly dawn when I realize—standing at our apartment door—that I've left the chicory outside. I'm not going back for it, so I knock. Papi's definitely up because I hear the TV. It's *Leave It to Beaver*, one of the few shows that make him laugh. His eyes are just as big and round and worried as I expect them to be when he opens the door and finds me there.

"Mi'ja! Por Dios, what's happened? What are you doing out there?" He reaches for me.

"Nothing, Papi. I'm fine. I went to put a bill in the mail and forgot my key." I brush right past him so that his eyes will not fully absorb me. Because one day that's going to happen. He'll look at me so hard, there'll be nothing left.

"But when did you go out?" He sounds horror stricken.

"Everything's fine, Papi. Tumba eso."

He goes to the kitchen and begins taking things out of the refrigerator and smacking them down on the counter. He's not having my story, but that's okay. He'll get nothing more from me.

After breakfast, I shower, then head for the living room to comb my hair. No mirrors today. It's time for *Perry Mason*, but the television is quiet. "Papi?" I say. He sits at the dining table, the paper from the trunk smooth and flat before him. I see now that it's a page torn from a book. He sniffles and stares out the window.

"What is it?" I ask, afraid.

"A poem," he says. "It's that damned Communist, Neruda." He slides the paper my way. Four stanzas have been underlined in faded pencil. I read:

Tonight I can write the saddest lines.
To think that I do not have her. To feel that I have lost her.

To hear the immense night, still more immense without her.
And the verse falls to the soul like dew to the pasture.

What does it matter that my love could not keep her.
The night is starry and she is not with me.

This is all. In the distance someone is singing. In the distance.
My soul is not satisfied that it has lost her.

Two, three more times I read Neruda's words and finally glance at my father. His head droops limply, the loosening skin of his face angling for the earth. "No," he says so softly I turn my right ear toward him. He looks up at me. He looks old. "Mi'ja, why would a man belabor such things?" He lays his forehead on the table. "It was a curse after all."

"*Papi*, Neruda is nothing to us. *Look . . .*" And I squeeze the poem into a tight ball, so tight that the words will never again align, never mean anything. Papi lifts his head to watch as I throw the paper away. Then I unhook the cord holding up the rest of the chicory and let it all cascade to the floor. I am surprised to find myself stomping and mashing the last of it into the linoleum. Whether it renders me invisible as I kick and grind, I don't know or care.

"Mi'ja, be careful," Papi musters. "Don't strain."

Puffing a little, I walk over and place my hand on my father's shoulder. It feels narrow. "That's done," I say. "Let's not think about it anymore—not Neruda, or loss, or loneliness, or any of it. What good does it do? That kind of thinking can only make us crazy."

Papi nods, and I ruffle his hair.

On the television, Raymond Burr beckons, so we go to the living room, turn up the volume, and take our seats.

THE MUSTACHE

MARITZA HAD AGREED TO MARRY ME, BUT ONLY IF I GREW a mustache. At first I found it hurtful that something so superficial should check her love for me. I remember the gibbous moon reflecting in Havana Harbor, the Malecón quiet as a death watch at that hour. This was 1902, before cars rattled their metal bones day and night along the boulevard. Outdoor concerts we called retretas drew large crowds in those days, and breathless couples danced polite versions of the danzón, or sometimes an American two-step, right out in the road. Maritza and I had danced all evening, then drifted toward the seawall as the musicians stowed their instruments, a fiddle string softly plunking.

Beguiling in white, Maritza laughed when I showed her the ring. "First, you must grow a mustache," she said, and touched my lips. I laughed too, believing she was joking, but her face grew serious. "I mean it, Martín. I won't marry a man with a bald lip, like a boy." She lifted her chin and puffed out her chest. "Quiero un hombre viril . . . but tender too," she said, "like José Martí. Like you, my love. Anyway, mira. Look at your hairy hands. You could grow a mustache in a week!"

My gorilla hands clutching her small smooth ones looked repellent to me. I shoved them into my pockets and turned my brooding on the ocean. My first wife, Eleanor, had made fun of my hairiness, my darkness, calling me a peasant— good-naturedly, you understand, but then she was a yanqui and fair. Maritza is dark like me and beautiful as the wind and stars. If she wanted me to grow more hair, if it meant that much to her, why wouldn't I oblige?

"You don't really mind, do you, Martín?" She lay her head on my shoulder, breathing against my neck until I felt like a block of wax left out in the Havana sun. A fruit seller on his way home stopped his little cart, the palm fronds he used for a roof rustling in the breeze. Maritza sifted through the mameys, a wrinkle forming between her eyebrows. Her family owned a sprawling fruit farm in Quivicán, just east of Havana, and Maritza never looked more authoritative than when pressing a guava or turning a mango this way and that. Finally, she chose one, removed her glove, and with her thumbnail scraped away a bit of the dun skin to reveal the red flesh beneath. It looked as if the mamey were bleeding. With a nod, she handed it back to the seller to cut.

Her lips grew shiny as she ate, and every so often she offered me a slice, but I wouldn't steal one bite from her eager mouth. She loved it so. One by one she flung the peels into the harbor, her shapely arm sweeping in a half arc as if she were tossing flowers to admirers. Standing there in the moonlight, the vast Atlantic sparkling before her, Maritza looked to me like the queen of Cuba. Her name means "of the sea," as if she, like the island, had arisen from the deep. Her name also means "bitter."

When the mamey was gone, she kissed my jaw and laughed at the stickiness she'd left behind. Only half meaning it, I grumbled and groaned until she tilted my head back and used her glove to wipe away the residue, wisps of her long hair grazing my chin. I felt myself smiling up into the sky where gauzy fingers of silver clouds reached across the moon. Far away, the echo of someone laughing.

Of course I would grow a mustache for her.

Maritza was right. The hair came in fast and thick, glossy as silk, black as the sea. I would be mustached in no time. We would wed, un milagro para mí. After Eleanor died of yellow fever, I worried the loping wretchedness of my grief would pursue me to the grave. Eleanor was buried in my family cemetery in Matanzas, where a marble statue of La Cachita stands guard. To appease her American father, we laid her to rest facing north. I left bouquets of laurel and roses, traced her name with my finger. Years passed. Inside me, a dark hollow widened. But then I met Maritza and love once more pumped through my veins.

Two weeks after I'd stopped shaving my lip, I studied my face in the mirror, intrigued by the new cast of it. When I pivoted to my right, I looked like Tío Garza, the one who used to tell ghost stories that scared the unholy hell out of my brother and me when we were kids. "Pleased to meet you," I said to my reflection, and laughed, the mustache arching like a frightened cat. Next to it, my teeth looked white as tombstones. Not bad, I thought, and imagined kissing Maritza on our wedding day, the mustache tickling her nose. If I were a woman, I don't think I'd want to kiss a mustache. Still, if any woman knew her own mind, Maritza did, and that settled it. So I combed the hairs smooth and flat, applied a few drops of the conditioning oil my barber had given me, and went to bed.

Next morning, as always, my neighbor's randy rooster crowed me awake. Cuban roosters are rangy, and this bird was smaller still, so I always marveled at the volume of its trumpeting: little ruffled man straining until his eyes bulged. I drowsed in bed half considering these points when I smelled La Rose Jacqueminot, the perfume Eleanor used to wear. It hung so heavily in the room, I pulled at the neck of my nightshirt and threw open the window, but the fresh air managed only a small incursion against it. I had not breathed that scent since the funeral, when it wafted up from the casket. The intimacy of it in my bedchamber, stealing beneath the wide legs of my pajama pants, whispering through my hair, disquieted me, so I stripped off my shirt, not even pausing to unbutton it, and went to the lavatory to wash up.

Right away, I saw the trouble. My mustache was gone. In the sink, a forest of black hairs, dollops of foam, and a blade still soiled from its task. Not a single whisker remained on my face.

Had I sleepwalked? That seemed the most reasonable explanation, but I couldn't believe it. Never in my life had I sleepwalked. My brother, when he was eight, would regularly arise in the night, sound asleep, and eat all the guava jelly and cheese in the house, or sometimes he would open the lid of the toy box our father had made for us and urinate there, thinking he had found the outhouse. But I had no such history.

Sweat pooled beneath my arms and on my chest, and if that damned rooster didn't stop shrieking, I thought I might wring its bony neck. I checked every room in the flat for signs of an intruder: kitchen, parlor, my little library (kettle, bowl of oranges, sofa, pillows, books), but nothing was amiss. It occurred to me then that my shaving soap contained peppermint oil, so I smelled my hands for evidence of my midnight shave, but they smelled like nothing at all, or maybe faintly of La Rose Jacqueminot.

Maritza and I had agreed to meet for lunch that day, and the question of how she would react worried me more than I care to admit. As a man, I probably should have demanded her hand unconditionally. Yes or no. Mustache or no mustache. What will it be, Maritza? But that's not my way.

That morning she had sent a note setting the time and place of our meeting. *I cannot wait to see the progress!* it said. To think of how proud I'd been, just twelve hours earlier, of my mustache's singular thickness and sheen. Not even that yanqui show-off, Teddy Roosevelt, boasted a better one. For that matter, neither did José Martí. Now I had only this naked strip of flesh to offer. I was ashamed.

"What happened?" She sat down, one hand gloved, the other unsheathed and frozen midair, black eyes curious but untroubled.

"I . . . I am not sure, Maritza. I awoke to find myself in this state." I kept touching my lip, as if the mustache were hiding there somewhere, but not even a patch of stubble remained, only a baldness that felt silly and childish.

The ocean breeze flicked a ribbon of hair across Maritza's face. In those days, she used a series of pins and combs to restrain the great fall of her hair, but it always broke free, which I liked. She ignored the wavering strand, sat back, and slackened, one by one, the fingers of her glove. So composed, my Maritza. How could I not admire this woman?

"Do you still intend to grow a mustache, Martín?"

I nodded. "That's my intent."

"And you'll tell me nothing more?"

"Nothing to tell." I looked out at the sea, the engineering marvel of the Malecón beating back the tide.

Maritza glanced around the sunny terrace, and the light made visible the fine freckles that swept the bridge of her nose. Behind her, the wind in the palms sent dark cloaks of shadow floating over the bricks. "I don't know what you're about, my love," she finally said, "but take your time. Handle this however you must. I don't mind waiting for you." She smiled. "Now, what are you eating? I want tuna."

❖   ❖   ❖

A slick pink scar arcs like Cuba itself across my right cheek. I did not acquire it as a boy climbing trees or swinging a machete into a stand of sugarcane for a stolen treat. I did not have it during my marriage with Eleanor. She admired the evenness of my skin even as we both understood its complexion meant she could never return to the States as my wife. Race rules were far laxer in Cuba. "You may be dark," she once said, "but you're the handsomest man I've ever known." I suppose that thrilled me more than it should have. Vanity is absurd in a man.

No, the scar came later, after my betrothal to Maritza—the consequence of my last best plan to gratify and thereby marry the woman I love. I had tried repeatedly to grow the mustache; each time, about seven days into the effort, I awoke in the same condition as before: La Rose Jacqueminot suffocating me, lip hairless as an egg, and the sink full of whiskers, every one a shiver of my decaying future with Maritza. I tried staying up all night. I slept at a friend's or relative's house (saying my flat was being painted or repaired). I even—through no small effort—obtained a pair of handcuffs and locked myself to the bed frame, well beyond the reach of the lavatory. I then tossed the key far enough across the room that I would have to drag the iron bed some three feet just to free myself. But all these strategies failed. As soon as I was once again mustached and ready to show myself to Maritza, I'd awaken shorn, my senses drowning in that poisonous perfume and shaving foam all over the sink or even my pillow.

I was in a secret hell, not daring to share the particulars with anyone. Initially amused, Maritza viewed my struggle as evidence I disliked the look of my mustached face, and while being thought conceited humiliated me, it also bought time.

⸙   ⸙   ⸙

When Eleanor and I were courting, she often asked me to take her to Havana's graveyards. The Spanish put their graveyards just outside cities, along the routes by which the greatest number of travelers would make their approach. This was to scare away the ill-intentioned, warn strangers that death comes to us all, but most ominously to the wicked. "Deliciously spooky," Eleanor called them, "but also beautiful." "If I were dead," she once said, "I'd want to roam here forever." I thought little of her words at the time, took them merely for dramatic exuberance, but they returned to me during the trouble with my mustache. Especially in the evenings, after dinner, when darkness came, my mind replayed our graveyard forays all those years ago and how they had rushed the blood to Eleanor's pale cheeks.

Her father had come down from los Estados Unidos to work on the Malecón and employed me as a surveyor. He was a lead engineer who ordered men about with a quiet voice, a wave of his hand, and everything was done without question. His authority, as they say, preceded him. Eleanor, too, expected compliance with her wishes, but she had a talkative, teasing way about her that added charm to the paternal equation. Not to mention her beauty.

When she wanted to visit the graveyards, she would say, "Show me the dead, Martín." Always a command, but with a pretty smile that came to you like a gift. It was a privilege to oblige her. In the intense light of Cuba's equatorial days, Eleanor's skin looked so white the only color my memory will assign to it is cold. But she was best in the lunar nights: glowing like a sprite, tripping among the tombstones, fearless, euphoric in a way I indulged but should not have. The first time she called me her "darling peasant," I nearly objected, but then she stepped over a low grave and proffered her hand. When I took it, she bent forward and kissed my palm with such tenderness that I could only embrace her. We danced a fragment of a popular waltz, me humming, Eleanor laughing. It was irreverent of us to be there in such a gay mood. I knew better, and perhaps that's why, later, I was tormented in that way, all my future happiness with Maritza in jeopardy.

In contemplating my time with Eleanor, I conceived a plan to end my torment. I had grown convinced it was Eleanor, or some Eleanor-inflected apparition, who shaved off my mustache every few days. While I'd never believed in ghosts, in light of the facts, what alternative did I have? Her presence had become no less real to me than that pathetic rooster strutting and hollering like he owned the morning. Eleanor's scent had settled into every crevice of my rooms and lodged in my nostrils so that wherever I went, I smelled La Rose Jacqueminot and suffered sinus headaches. There was no denying that Eleanor had returned to plant her yanqui flag once more in my heart.

And Maritza's patience had begun to wear thin. She sent me a note that said only, *I did not think it was so much to ask.* When I read it, I pounded my dining table and upset a coffee cup. But then I buttoned my vest, put on a fresh collar, and went to the window to wait for night. Once it was dark, I packed my shaving tackle—razor, strop, brush, cup, and soap—into its leather pouch, filled a flask with hot coffee, and made my way to Eleanor's favorite cemetery: El Cementerio de Cristóbal Colón, or, as she called it, Christopher Columbus Cemetery. Awaiting a cab at that late hour, I found the night air unusually chill, even for December, and noticed tendrils of fog crawling along the grass, heaving in halos of light cast by streetlamps. A breeze made me tremble, but I was also—I can admit this now—afraid. Yes, anger drove me, but from the gloom, fear blinked its yellow eyes.

If you've never visited El Cementerio de Cristóbal Colón, you can't imagine what it's like to come upon such an imposing memorial to death in the middle of the night. A majestic trio of stone archways marks the entrance, each tall and wide enough to make a man feel he had entered a land of giants. Beyond the main gate, the cemetery, with its soaring statues and monuments, advances like a tidal wave, all 122 acres of it. When the moon broke from the clouds, the marble faces of angels and saints gleamed in the half-light, the points of their white wings sharp against the blue-black sky. Perhaps they will watch over me, I thought. Then a cloud or the fog would steal them away, and once more I found myself alone with my shaving tackle tucked under my arm and a flask of coffee knocking against my leg as I walked among the mausoleums.

The architect, Loira, designed El Colón on a grid, like a miniature city, with neighborhoods and districts. He meant to keep the classes separate, even after death. No reprieve for those born to disadvantage. Somewhere in a quiet corner with tall trees, tangles of moss dripping from their limbs, I'd find Eleanor's favorite grave site. I couldn't remember the name of the family, only those lissome trees and the way they secreted the spot from the rest of the cemetery.

The Velázquez family—I found them at last, one of the humbler mausoleums in Colón Cemetery, but a mausoleum nonetheless. It housed the tombs of a mother, father, and two children, all of whom had died in a cholera epidemic. Eleanor would sit on the low stone wall and smile up at me as if la muerte weren't all around us. Sometimes bats danced overhead, hunting mosquitoes. I'd urge her home, threaten to abandon her there if she didn't accompany me, but there was no bending her will.

From an iron bench I brushed twigs and shooed a green lizard, sluggish in the cool air. Then I laid out my shaving tackle, lingering over the blade glinting in the fitful moonlight, and took a drink of steaming coffee. It burned my tongue. I shook my head and laughed, but not so much at the burn as at the absurdity of my predicament. You think your life is unfurling in a certain way, and you let yourself grow happy about it, a smile rising at the slightest thing. A boy in short pants eating a pastelito makes you grin like a lunatic at the vision of your own hoped-for children, their dark shiny heads rising, year by year, from the Cuban earth, your wife towering behind them, kind and wise. Then you find yourself in a midnight cemetery guarding your mustache from the covetous ghost of an American woman you once loved. Who wouldn't laugh?

Hours passed. The breeze died. A slow sheet of fog wrapped me in white. It was then I feared I had made a mistake. I loved Maritza and had come to Colón Cemetery to fight for my future with her, but I won't deny I feared dying. As I consider the matter now, it seems obvious that if Eleanor had sought my blood, she'd already had countless opportunities to drive the blade into my carotid and watch my life pour out. Even so, in the cemetery, every owl call and rustle in the undergrowth seemed to portend death. Eventually, I lay down on my little bench and pulled my knees up as far as I could to keep warm, sometimes propping myself up on an elbow to sip. Waiting. When I could fight it no longer, I nodded off amid visions of Eleanor returned from the grave to play about my neck with a sharp blade.

I awoke! The fog had laid hold of me. How else can I say it? I found the cold form of it clasping my body, entwined among my arms and legs, and the razor's glint against my lip. At the realization that once more my mustache would be scraped away and I would be deprived of happiness and a future, I whipped my head sideways and lashed out. Never had or would I raise a hand against a woman, but I was not fighting a woman. That's when the razor's finely stropped edge sliced my cheek. It was a simple thing for it to do, the outcome as inexorable as falling when the ground gives way. Blood ran down my face, onto my clothing, even splattered the fog itself, or so it seemed. I reached and grabbed in vain, struggling to take hold of whatever it was, sometimes thinking I had found a wrist or a handful of hair, more often seeing my fingers, bloody and flexed, disappear into the fog.

"Eleanor!" I cried. "Let me go! I rise up against you!" Those words strike me now as strange, almost idiotic, but when I said them, my body shook, and I felt tears come to my eyes.

Something clinked against the pavement, and I looked down to see the gory razor blade next to my shoe, several drops of my own blood landing nearby. Each one made a perfect circle that the porous concrete drew out and away from itself until all that remained were feathery red stars.

By the time I'd staunched the bleeding and gathered my tackle, morning had broken and the fog began to dissipate. For the first time in a month, I did not smell La Rose Jacqueminot with every inhalation. What welcome drafts of air those were. After a short rest on the bench, I stood to leave and heard nearby the clang of metal against stone, and behind that, a softer sound: a woman sobbing. At first I worried Eleanor had devised some new way to oppress me, but I walked toward the sound and found an old señora, all in black, on her knees, forehead pressed to the damp ground. When she rose to a kneeling position, she reached up and rapped a large, hinged ring, like a doorknocker, three times against the marble tomb. Weeping all the while, she sometimes rocked herself, a mourner come to plead at the grave of the young mother, La Milagrosa. So much despair in this world, so many disappointments. I wonder how we bear it. If not for my bloodied appearance, I would have given her my coffee.

As a consequence of my night in El Colón, I bear now the oddest scar. As I said before, the shape is much like that of the island, but it lacerates my mustache so that the right third is partitioned from the rest by a shiny pink disfigurement Maritza cannot tolerate the look of. She admires my mustache's thick black luster but will always, I think, view it as ruined. In fact, she will only sit, stand, or talk to me on my left side, for she cannot see the scar from that vantage.

Our children, who have never known me otherwise, think

nothing of their papi's Cuba-shaped scar, but Maritza laments what might have been. Every once in a while, when we're strolling along the Malecón or lounging after dinner, she refuses to look at me at all, or when she does, appears to see through me to some more solid thing beyond my ken. At those times, when solitude settles a cool vapor right down inside me, I insist I will shave and be done with it, but Maritza says, "No," and touches my arm.

PLAGUE LOVE

"TAKES A LITTLE GETTING USED TO, DOESN'T IT?" THE
mask muffled his voice, but she could hear the resolve. He
was good-natured. He wasn't complaining. "Where'd you
get them?"

"Online," she said, fidgeting. She wanted to pull her legs
up onto the bench, crisscross applesauce like she was a kid
again and this—the two of them in hazmat suits, the empty
park, the crows tossed against a Parrish blue sky—was light-
hearted fun. But the suits were meant to be disposable and felt
as if they'd easily rip. They both noticed the flimsiness.

"Weren't they expensive?" Arms aloft, feet lifted, he examined the papery white material covering nearly every inch of
him, every inch of her, all but the goggled eyes. "How much?"

"Too much," she said with a shrug.

"I'll help pay. I have some money left, and I can try to sell
the Triumph."

"Motorcycles *are* kinda dangerous," she said, gingering her
head until, from the corner of her eye, she could see him nodding. It felt impossible to turn all the way. The fabric would

surely give, especially where the hood met the neckline. So they kept pivoting toward each other, stiff as tree trunks, eyes furtive. This was for the best anyway. It had been a while, and they felt almost shy now. From a distance, they might have been strangers waiting for a bus.

Shoulder by shoulder, they watched the crows glide. Beyond the black sails of their wings, silver clouds mounted— their crisp edges unequivocal, like they knew what they were about. The sky purpled toward evening, and a breeze upset the October maple leaves, tumbled them together with assorted trash. A dirty Styrofoam cup settled at their feet. He nudged it.

She nudged it too and said, "It'll outlive us all."

From their bench, they surveyed the park and a far scattering of houses, but the crows and a few frenetic squirrels were the only living things in sight.

He stood up and began to pace. After several rounds, he stopped, searched the sky, and groaned, his fingertips briefly gripping his head. She studied her feet and tried not to cry.

When he noticed her that way, he said, "I'm okay. We're okay," and thought to squat at her knees but reconsidered—the fabric again, so thin. Instead, he straightened his back, stiffened his arms, and began lumbering goofily to and fro. "Hey," he said, "I'm the Stay-Puft Marshmallow Man!"

She watched him, his goggles winking in the low light. "You *look* like the Stay-Puft Marshmallow Man." She laughed.

"You look like a snow queen," he said.

"You look like a spaceman," she said, so he took giant slow-motion steps, and his eyes grew big and serious with the effort. They laughed harder.

"You look like . . . a cloud," he said, puffing in the mask.

"You look like the Pillsbury Doughboy." But not really. He was a slender man, the hazmat hanging from his lean frame.

"You look like a . . ." He paused. "I'm out." But he'd nearly said, "Ghost."

◍   ◍   ◍

The crows hollered, a grumpy row of them crowding the power line, old-man hunched and swaying in the breeze. He sat down, but sideways this time, facing her, one leg hinged hard, the hazmat straining at the knee. "I wish I could take you out to dinner," he said. "I know it's old-fashioned, but that's what I want. You in a silk dress. Pearls."

"Pearls?" By degrees, she turned to face him, gentling her limbs like prayer beads to protect the suit.

"Paradise to me."

Black lashes ringed her black eyes, and he could just glimpse her thick brows below the hazmat shrouding her forehead. She used to pluck them, but now they met in the middle, and he found himself drawn to this bit of hair. It made her look like a Tajik bride. He could not precisely recall her nose just then, and her mouth waded through the fog of his memory as a cherry or strawberry, which struck him as ridiculous and wrong. But her eyes and those brows—they could be enough.

"Where would we go?" She reached her gloved hand toward him, and he clasped it in both of his, waited for their bodies' warmth to bleed through.

"What's your pleasure?"

She scanned the horizon, and the setting sun conjured copper from her irises. "Shawarma?"

"Sure."

"Jeweled rice?"

"Yes!"

"Künefe?"

"Absolutely."

"And dancing," she said, eyes narrowing and the mask crawling upward with the smile he couldn't see. "Slow and dreamy."

"I'd dazzle you with a fancy gift," he said. "Emeralds?"

"That *is* old-fashioned." She rolled her eyes. "But I can top it." This with a wink. "What I want most is the rubies of your lips warm against mine, sweet like caramel with an oaky wine note at the back."

"Oh *no*." He laughed and, through his bootie, toed a silvery gum wrapper, the red tide of leaves surging and retreating around them. "That's the worst," he said, and brought her hand to his mask, kissed the antiseptic fabric with a smack so she'd know what he was doing in there. "I miss you," he said.

"I know," she said. "Me too."

"This is hard."

"It'll be okay." She nodded, trying to believe herself.

"I want to make love with you," he said.

The crows had finally gone to bed, and the park drifted into a deeper quietude.

"Make love with your eyes." She squeezed his hand.

"How does that work?"

"Eyes are the windows of the soul." She'd always admired the particular gray of his, not light but dark and winsome as the Black Sea of her childhood. Perhaps, in this foundering world, they would show her the way.

"Do you see my eyes loving you?"

"I do," she said.

Release

SHOELACE,

CAMISOLE,

ROPE

YULIA CUPPED HER FACE AGAINST THE GLASS TO BLOCK out the Florida sun. The breeze hesitated and she'd begun to sweat, wisps of dark hair sticking like sideburns. She was choosing her favorite, preparing to make a deal. It was a serious business. Before her, in the bakery's display window, a spread of unfathomable bounty: cakes, napoleons, fluffy things blushing with pale pink sugar. Even apple tarts. What exotic ecstasy they would be. What she wouldn't give for a single bite. She had never tasted an apple. A boy at her school in Camagüey had once bragged about his father smuggling in a whole box of them. Said he'd eaten his fill, each one so crisp it nearly cracked his teeth. No one believed him.

She salivated and glanced down the plaza's crumbling walkway, past the potted palms and Kiko's sandwich shop, finally focusing on the busy supermarket. Any minute now, Abuela would come out of the Winn-Dixie, and she wouldn't like to find Yulia drooling over all that Américan caca.

But to Yulia, everything after the snarling dogs and towering black Atlantic of their midnight bolt from Mariel was a kind of fairyland: los Estados Unidos, Miami, and now this bakery. And not a bakery but a village of buttercream-spackled houses with cherry chimneys, coconut shingles, and puff pastry foundations. Though she was old enough to know better, Yulia nearly found herself searching out the tiny blue Smurfs of the show she sneaked Saturday mornings.

When she was eight, she and Abuela had taken the train to Santiago to visit the cloud forest. Local legend had it the place was enchanted, home to glass-winged butterflies and elves. Yulia had gotten her hopes up, but all that she found there was a lot of rank vegetation and frogs. Cuba—Yulia never had thought much of it. But this new land, the United States of bakeries and apple tarts—that was a different matter.

The breeze rose again, trembled the palms and jangled a garland of seashells someone had strung outside the sandwich shop. Yulia wiped her breath from the glass and flipped the nuisance of her braid over her shoulder, the thick black line of it snaking down her back. Through the frame of her hands, she studied each pastry, imagined its heft and aroma, the texture of it on her tongue, slipping down her throat.

Back in Camagüey, long before the Mariel boatlift, there were rations. Among them, two pounds of sugar per month for her and Abuela to share. With it, Abuela had cobbled together the typical guajiro dessert: makeshift rice pudding minus vanilla, cinnamon, even eggs most times. And the milk came canned from Hungary. Little charm in a soggy bowl of rice overbloomed with sweet, metallic milk, but Yulia had eaten it. In Cuba, she had always been hungry enough to eat, always craved sweets.

These exotic Américan pastries had to taste like Heaven.

Anyway, Cuba was a thing behind her now. To dwell on it at this point—with their new life in Miami, in Raúl's garage apartment—would be like walking backward forever and ever.

Was that Abuela? No. Abuela was smaller, stood up straighter, her whole body a study in vigilance. Soon she'd emerge beaming with her precious plantains, chicken, rice, and a great sack of Goya black beans. Good food, she'd say. Cuban food. None of that yanqui mierda that makes you fat and stupid. Comelóns, Abuela called Américans, greedy pigs. And Yulia knew what this meant: no bologna, no Wonder bread or mayonnaise, and no apples. Abuela considered apples the symbolic heart of yanqui badness. Pure poison.

But the grandmother especially prohibited all things sweet—Oreos, Twinkies, Sno Balls—everything Yulia would have put on the grocery list if Abuela ever asked her . . . which she didn't. To Abuela, sugar was the sacred corazón of Cuba, and real Cubans would abhor any not conjured from the island's fertile womb. Yulia would get no sugar in her tea or on her cereal. At the refugee center, Abuela had allowed her several of the greasy hamburgers the Catholics proffered in crinkly cartooned paper, but brushed away the pale hand offering a frosted sugar cookie. Yulia had wanted to cry.

Now, in Miami, Abuela hid a signed picture of el Jefe Máximo in her underwear drawer. In Cuba, this same portrait had hung in the living room of the tiny apartment she and Yulia shared. The grandmother had not wanted to come to los Estados Unidos. When Fidel opened up Mariel, it was her nephew Raúl who talked her into leaving. Raúl's mother, Diana, was dying in Miami. Didn't Abuela want to see her own sister again before it was too late?

It had been twenty-three years and a revolution since the sisters last saw each other. Abuela longed to kiss Diana's forehead, to hold her hand and laugh with her over old things. And in the end, she and Yulia betrayed Fidel. Left Cuba. They became gusanos, their very neighbors pelting them with eggs the night they slunk away. Even Abuela wondered where Cubans had suddenly found such abundance.

But Yulia, not Diana, had been the reason they left.

The apple tart—that was Yulia's choice. Definitely. Not pretty, but utterly beguiling with its glistening sugar and mysterious amber fruit. Time was short, and Yulia had no money. She jiggled her skinny leg and fussed with the braid Abuela had torqued too tightly. *What I wouldn't give*, she thought. *What I wouldn't give.* She felt in her pockets but found them empty. She knew this already.

Still no Abuela.

Yulia looked herself over, then again at her feet, something there. She kicked away a few flattened cigarette butts, then bent down, loosened one of her purple shoelaces, whipped it from her shoe, and wadded it into a tight bundle. Stuffed into the corner where the glass met a brick ledge, the shoelace wanted only to be taken up in a new way, maybe by a bird building a nest. "There you go," she said to no one, and rushed toward Abuela, who was just coming through the Winn-Dixie's automatic doors. The blast of frozen air swept Yulia's hot skin and made her shiver.

⁕ ⁕ ⁕

It didn't take long for Abuela to notice the shoe. "Where's the string?" Half question, half accusation.

"Fell out, I think." Yulia had begun lying. It was the only way with Abuela, especially now, in América, where the grandmother stood sentry over all things Cuban—Yulia most of all. She figured she'd give up lying later, when she became an adult and ran her own life, but until then, it felt like a necessity.

"Hmph." Abuela packed beans and rice into an empty margarine container for Yulia's lunch. "We don't have any more. You should have been careful."

"I know."

"Well, you better find a way to keep it on your foot before you leave or I'm going to put some duct tape." She nodded at the shoe, the hook of her nose carving the air.

Yulia rushed to her room. She would not go to school with duct tape on her shoe. Only recently had the kids stopped calling her a Marielita and asking if she had tuberculosis or venereal disease. The change came unexpectedly. During recess, by the monkey bars, a popular girl had openly praised Yulia's long thick rope of hair.

"You could sell it for at least a thousand dollars," the girl had said, her authority impressive. "But you should use a ribbon on your braid. Your hair's too pretty for a ratty rubber band."

After that, the Marielita remarks quieted. After that, all the girls admired Yulia's hair and conjectured together that there must have been something magical in the Cuban air of her birth.

But there were no ribbons in the apartment, not for hair or a makeshift shoelace, no more shoes that weren't sandals or flip-flops either. No excess in their small world. Yulia eventually found a wide rubber band that she cut and wound through the holes for a lace. Still embarrassing, but better than duct tape.

Abuela handed her the lunch and eyed her handiwork. "Resourceful," she said, and she kissed Yulia goodbye.

⦚　⦚　⦚

Not nearly enough on the list to warrant a trip to the Winn-Dixie, but they were going for Diana. Abuela would prepare a sopa de ajo to cleanse her blood. Raúl, who'd come for lunch and to drop off some of his daughter's old clothes for Yulia, scoffed at Abuela's plan, said soup with forty cloves of garlic or whatever wouldn't cure anything except kissing. Abuela told him not to talk to her like she was some crazy curandera. "Cubans know science, Raúl. Garlic brings down inflammation. Too bad you don't know that." Raising her voice wasn't her way, but she could muster a quiet severity that intimidated most everyone. Raúl had once joked about his tía being a female Che, but Abuela said the revolution was nothing to joke about and left the room.

Among her cousin's cast-offs, Yulia spied a camisole: pale pink with cream lace along the neckline, like new. She'd longed for a training bra at least but was so flat chested as to not yet require one. This camisole would be a nice substitute, so she snatched it up before Abuela had a chance to inspect the pile of donated clothing—her mantis hands rotating each item—and announce what Yulia would and would not be allowed to wear.

Together they bounced and swayed with the bus's sloppy

cornering, Yulia's knobby knee colliding with Abuela's fuller one. The contrast roused in the grandmother a familiar concern. *Too skinny. Frail*: the word felt like fear.

Days before the boatlift, Raúl had called her. It was the apartment building's only phone, one of precious few in all of Camagüey. Abuela remembered how the receiver shook in her hand, forbidden Miami on the other end. "Think of *her*," Raúl had said. "Think of Yulia."

No one thought of Yulia more than she did. Yulia, who was sallow and sometimes ran fevers. A sickly constitution, the Cuban doctors said, but Abuela couldn't help thinking a few more chickens in the pot would begin to mend her poor health, and the handful of rangy pollos that paced the roads of Camagüey hardly counted. It was for Yulia that Abuela abandoned Cuba.

The bus—supposedly air-conditioned—felt swampy and smelled of oniony sweat and violet water. Raúl had offered to drive them to the store, but Abuela preferred the bus. "With the people," she said.

"Whatever that means," Raúl replied with a laugh. Abuela didn't laugh.

The engine whined, and Yulia shifted her weight on the bench seat, her hand coming to rest against her grandmother's leg. Outside, afternoon thunderheads arranged themselves like snowy mountains in the sky. Yulia studied them and tried to imagine a world made of ice.

"At the store, maybe we should get Diana a pastry?" she ventured. "Maybe an apple tart?" Then a lie: "My teacher said apples cure a lot of different diseases, I think even what Diana has." But she had no idea what ailed her great-aunt.

Abuela turned to her, and Yulia found her own young

eyes in her grandmother's old ones. In a voice pitched high, Abuela said, "Are you crazy?" Maybe the question sounded rude, but Yulia knew what she meant: that she was smart enough to understand that Abuela's position on the evils of yanqui sweets would never change. They were bad enough for healthy people. "Can you imagine," Abuela said, mouth bending downward, "what that shit could do to poor Diana? To anyone . . . not strong?"

Yulia nodded but imagined instead what it would be like to have a whole tart to herself: flowers blooming from her toes and fingers, each blink of her lashes dusting her cheeks with gold pollen. Buzzing and spellbound, honeybees would flock to her sweetness.

As soon as Abuela got in the checkout line, Yulia skipped down to the bakery, jittery about the shoelace. She searched the ledge and all around, but it was gone. That was good news in a way. Someone or something had found her offering acceptable. On the other hand—no apple tart had come to her. Not yet, at least. But there they were, a whole ridge of them flaky brown and beckoning behind the frosted elfin village. *What I wouldn't give.*

Yulia thought fast. She could pull out her other shoelace, but that would only bate Abuela's fury. Anyway, and more importantly, maybe it wasn't enough. Maybe that's why she hadn't gotten her tart. One dirty purple shoelace could hardly buy ambrosia. What could she spare this time? Shoes? Shorts? Underwear? Her Underdog T-shirt—the one Abuela disdained and only allowed her to wear after Yulia explained that the cartoon came from Russian folklore? (It didn't.) Then it came to her: satiny blush with lace and making Yulia feel fantastically grown up. She was loath to part with the camisole so soon, *but for the tart . . . think of the tart!* Could she slip out of it while keeping her shirt on? Could she leave it there for the whole world to see? Abuela would be none the wiser. That was one mercy.

Yulia glanced around: a lady in pink curlers pushing a cart across the parking lot, an old man reading the paper and bobbing to the reggae rhythm drifting from his car radio. The bakery cashier bustled between the counter and the back, where she disappeared from view. "Next time she goes," Yulia whispered. And then she was gone. So Yulia reached through the armholes of her shirt, pulled first one, then the other camisole strap down over her elbows and slipped her hands through. Disrobing in this way, so that anyone could see her, shot a thread of electricity down her legs. In a flash, the camisole whisked over Yulia's head, and before Abuela came out to find her, made a fetching pink parcel folded like a hankie and deposited on the bakery's ledge, the bricks rough against young fingertips. "Here," she said, "and just to be clear, it's *for the apple tart.*"

⫙   ⫙   ⫙

When Diana died, Abuela didn't cry, at least not that Yulia observed, but she grew quiet, spent hours alone in her room, stiffened when Yulia tried to hug away her sorrow. "I'm okay, Yulia," she said, her voice low, hands strong against her granddaughter's small shoulders. "Diana was old and sick. I knew this was coming. It's part of aging, nothing any of us can change."

"But it's sad, Tita," Yulia said, thinking, for the first time in her life, that her grandmother looked very old.

"It is."

Abuela went to the kitchen, Yulia following behind, and pulled from a high shelf the paella pan she'd found at Catholic Charities. "For the reception," she said. Raúl had told her not to bother herself, that in América, friends and distant relatives brought food for the family, but Abuela would hardly trust Yulia's health to strangers. At least there would be one dish her granddaughter could safely eat.

"I need some peppers and shrimps." Abuela set the pan on the counter. "More Bijol too." She looked at the clock and nodded toward the Winn-Dixie three miles away. "Go get ready," she said.

In her tiny bedroom, Yulia stood before the mirror deliberating. She did not know her great-aunt Diana except as a skeletal figure in Raúl's gauzy guestroom and felt little sadness at her passing. There was a bland sobriety in the face of death, but death as an idea more than as a resident of Yulia's life. Death the mysterious force that stiffened legions of dragonflies, a pet parrot, several half-bald fighting cocks, some balseros when they struck out madly across the Florida Straits. Death was a disappearing agent, but it had never disappeared anything Yulia missed. Sometimes she thought she missed parents, but not *her* parents especially. She'd never known them. As a consequence of this, and of being young, she thought far more of what she hoped to acquire than of what she feared to lose.

She was sorry for her grandmother, though. Abuela had lost her sister, had been part of a family before Yulia even existed. Improbable images came to her: of her grandmother as a little girl with her own mother and abuelita, maybe playing with her sister in the yard, the two of them brushing each other's hair. Diana's death must have grieved Abuela, but with a dolor that kept its dry belly to the ground like a lizard.

Yulia drew her long braid forward, fingered the frayed tip that reached down past her ribs. It had been two weeks since she gave up the camisole, and no apple tart had come of it. Now, they were off again to the Winn-Dixie, Abuela for the bits of Cuba she could still grasp, Yulia for her heart-of-América tart, a thing she'd come to need to a degree that surprised her. Perhaps one day, when she was older and wiser, she'd understand why.

All she knew this day was that another chance had come. If she could find a worthy currency, she'd tender a trade so tempting it could not be refused. But the bedroom offered nothing suitable: bedding, a torn Holly Hobbie poster, some clothes Abuela kept inventoried like an accountant, a few books. Nothing her grandmother wouldn't notice missing, and nothing that *felt* right. Yulia sought a treasure the pastry elves would value.

She looked again at the braid and agreed with the girls at school. It was pretty. But it had been part of her forever, swinging about her shoulders like a jump rope. From Camagüey, almost a year and three hundred miles behind her, the school-yard rhymes still echoed: girls and boys, guavas and mangos, tarantulas and zunzuncitos, innuendo and grinning, the jump rope turning faster and faster. But this was Miami, and it was time to move forward.

No scissors in the house. Abuela wouldn't buy anything she could borrow from Raúl. No matter. Yulia exchanged her tank top for a striped shirt with a kangaroo pocket, and into this pocket secreted a small paring knife. It nestled there perfectly, tapping against her flat stomach with each step toward the bus stop.

Even when she hid the knife, Yulia doubted she'd go

through with her plan. Giving up a shoelace or a bit of under-wear was one thing, but cutting off her hair was too much, the kind of too much that transformed regular girls into objects of whispered concern. She might as well fling herself into the ocean or burn her grandmother's picture of el Jefe. Abuela would think Yulia had gone mad if she came out of the Winn-Dixie to find her shorn like a spring sheep.

In salons all over Miami dwelled cool-handed beauticians who would lob off a girl's childish braid and plunk it in a keep-sake bag just for her, but Abuela liked Yulia's hair long. It was the granddaughter's only abundance, and the weight and shine of it sliding through Abuela's fingers satisfied her. Even in the Cuban torpor, where less hair might have been a relief, Yulia would stand on their mildewed balcony as Abuela snipped off one scant inch, never more, not even if Yulia begged. Add to this fact the funereal atmosphere making sacrilege of haircuts and apple tarts, and instinctively Yulia understood that what-ever she did, she was on her own.

When she found herself before the bakery, the offering of her camisole gone, knife in one hand, braid in the other, a feeling of absurdity came to her. This for *that*? A pastry? A bit of apple and butter? Flour and sugar? It's *that* important? But the reply mounted in her salivary glands, which tingled and flooded her mouth, made her swallow and swallow. Her legs felt swimmy. Sweat pooled at the back of her neck. Hun-gry, nearly starving, she drove the blade against her hair, back and forth, back and forth, each fiber emitting a tiny *tick* the moment it gave way.

When the braid tore free, Yulia felt taller, as if she were seeing the world from a little higher up. She laid the rope of hair on the brick ledge and walked back to the Winn-Dixie to wait for Abuela, the splayed ends of her new bob lifting in the storm-stirred air.

When Abuela gasped at what was left of Yulia's hair, Yulia began to cry, said she felt sick, hot, *so hot*, hotter than she'd ever been. "The hair was suffocating me, Tita. I couldn't stand it. I was on fire!" It was the worst lie she'd ever told.

Abuela's hands shook and the heaviest of the Winn-Dixie bags kept slipping off her hip. A roll of thunder and several splats of rain made Abuela duck her head. She told Yulia to grab onto her purse strap and led her over to the pay phone.

The grandmother's knobby fingers searched the purse for a dime, but her eyes watched Yulia. "Do you feel dizzy?" she asked.

Yulia shook her head no.

Then, into the receiver, "Raúl, por favor, come get us. Yulia's sick!"

By the time they reached the apartment, Yulia felt so ill she wondered if she'd lied at all. Heat and cold attacked her at once, and she was weepy, confused. Deep tides of guilt waved through her. To see Abuela this way—blanched, her iron composure shaken, fear widening her eyes—it was awful. The thermometer read 100 degrees. Abuela shook her head, but Raúl insisted Yulia was probably just dehydrated and brought Gatorade from the house. Abuela meanwhile struggled to peel a coconut, its water, she insisted, the best cure for dehydration. Through it all, Yulia lay on the sofa sinking and sinking into its suffocating softness.

❖   ❖   ❖

By the day of the funeral, Yulia had officially recovered from—it had been decided—a bout of dehydration-induced delirium. Américan water, Abuela theorized, was not as nourishing as Cuban water. Maybe you had to drink more of it just to reap the same benefit. There had been questions, of course. A pocketknife, Yulia said, lying open on the window ledge at the bakery. An impulsive act. She'd hardly comprehended what she was doing.

Abuela sighed like she'd feared all along something like this would happen. "Estados Unidos," she said, as if that explained all bad things.

But it was time to lay Diana to rest, and the incident was set aside, not—Yulia absolutely understood this—forgotten. This event, like innumerable others, would be recorded on the vast register of Abuela's brain.

At the church, Raúl wept. Diana's friends wept. The priest spoke of paradise, and the rain drove against the stained glass, where a lizard skittered over the faces of the saints.

The reception broke upon Yulia like a magical tsunami. She'd never seen, never imagined anything like it. Five— she counted them—bundt cakes, eight flans, scores of guava pastelitos and pastelitos de carne, arroz con pollo, Abuela's paella, nearly everything Yulia could imagine eating. The great lot of it reclined on a series of tables arranged like train cars throughout the living and dining areas of someone's fancy house.

Abuela was talking with one of Diana's friends, and Yulia half listened as they waded through the crowd.

"Isn't this nice?" the woman said, her gray hair a little bit lavender under a skylight, gold jewelry winking from her neck, ears, and fingers.

"In Cuba," Abuela said, "we bury the dead in a cardboard box, then go home to mourn in private."

"This isn't Cuba." The woman smiled and pulled a crumpled Kleenex from her purse. "I brought Diana's favorite treat." She touched the corners of her reddening eyes. "Whenever I visited her, I would bring two: one for then and one for after I left. Sometimes it was all she could eat."

Abuela nodded, mouth set firm.

The friend looked at Yulia, said, "Here, honey. I'll show you where they are. Two dozen of the best tarte Tatin you'll ever taste. I buy them from that shop by the Winn-Dixie. Get one now before they're all gone!" And she guided Yulia to a corner table, white cloth draped over it, a vase of pink and purple roses, and a huge platter of apple tarts from the bakery where Yulia had bargained away her treasures.

Until that moment, she had only observed them through glass, never inhaled the buttery aroma that now whispered like a secret through the white living room, its tiled floor the color of beach sand.

Desire invaded every cell of her.

Diana's friend patted Yulia on the back and left her there with a perfect pyramid of apple tarts, not even one missing yet. The air-conditioning felt cold against Yulia's exposed neck. She liked this new coolness, the lightness above her shoulders. It made her stand up straighter. She turned her head more, too, just to feel the strands of hair move freely.

The tarts beckoned. Want flooded her mouth. *Really*, Yulia thought, *why not?* She'd paid thrice already. And they weren't poison. That was ridiculous. They weren't caca. *Why not?*

But she knew why not.

Across the room stood the proud staff of Abuela's body.

Her face was grim, eyes slanting toward fear. Guests brushed past her, mumbled words, paused briefly to see if she'd engage, but she only nodded stiffly and watched Yulia, the girl with the short black hair and skinny legs, nascent English. She looked tall. Was that new? And before the girl, a bloat of yanqui pastries.

When their eyes met, Abuela didn't say anything, didn't hold up a warning finger or shake her head, not even a tiny movement only Yulia would notice. Dead air filled the widening space between them. Maybe it was the house with its plastic slipcovers, its gaudy chandelier and white everything, maybe a trick of the light, but Abuela looked so small and shabby just then. The sight of her settled brick heavy in Yulia's chest, made her aware of drawing air in through her nose, pushing it back out through barely parted lips.

But if she concentrated, if she envisaged the rush of sweetness, she could manage these burdens, the choked breathing, the weight of it all. After a few moments, Yulia turned back to the table, long neck gracefully pivoting, and reached out her hand.

THE MOTH

DISGUSTED, MARI LEANED INTO THE LISTING CART, weaved up and down the rows past doughy patrons spread out on the floor like softening butter. Some had even removed their shoes, their repellent toes whisking the open air. All about them lay books and magazines in careless heaps. *What disrespect!* Bitter contempt lodged in Mari's throat, and she shook her head, as if the library were full of stinking fish fit only to be cast into the darkest trench of the sea.

In Cuba she had operated an independent library, lining up the colorful spines alongside jars of sofrito in her tiny kitchen. She knew every book's checkout history, who had smuggled it home, let it droop butterflied across their chest as they nodded off. She repaired the tattered bindings with tender fingers and homemade glue that smelled of pine, often glancing out her fourth-story window at clouds that morphed into sylphs. At night, when she lay down to sleep, she sniffed her disdain for the government that deemed her little library illegal, and, too, for other so-called independent librarians—usually men—whose collections merely fronted political dissention.

Heavy-handed buffoons, she thought them, *oblivious to the power of las palabras. Machete in one hand, pinga in the other. How would they hold a book? With their feet?*

❖   ❖   ❖

With cold-stiffened fingers, Mari pulled on her sweater. *Ridiculous*. It was July. In Florida. But something was wrong with the air-conditioning, and all anyone could do was shrug in dismay and halfhearted confusion.

"We aren't supposed to adjust the thermostat," one of the librarians explained, the large one with the wide mouth. Sydney was her name. "They have to take care of it in maintenance. Silly, isn't it?"—this with a laugh.

Mari nodded but thought, *Typical. Where was the woman's initiative? Such a milquetoast!* Still, it wasn't Mari's affair. She wasn't even a librarian. So she maneuvered the heavy cart down a quiet aisle and paused to button her sweater. Fingers working, her eyes sought the sky but found instead the textured ceiling, its menagerie of shapes: dragon, seagull. The sweater's bewitching softness made Mari linger at her task. In the Salvation Army, she had marveled that someone gave it up. A fabric so sublimely supple she sometimes liked to pull it on over bare skin, feel it glide across her breasts, caress the sharp corners of her shoulders. When had a man's hands been so elegant?

At day's end, Mari parked the empty cart and washed up. The books smelled musty and darkened her fingers with waxy filth. How long had she been in Miami? Three years? Four? Long enough for the memory of her Havana kitchen library to drift away from her. In its place, the gently gilded tale of a land where she had been queen and the books gathered to her breast smelled sweetly of oregano. The ones piled about her now seemed soulless and hollow as exoskeletons.

Mari folded the sweater neatly and stored it in an old metal locker someone had stashed in a closet at the back of the library, amidst other things deposed but still too good to throw out.

A quick tug on the padlock to ensure it had caught and Mari turned to go.

But then.

Something fluttering.

A moth.

Just at the corner of her vision.

A common gray one like you always see.

Knowing their insatiable hunger for sumptuous things, Mari lunged after it. But no matter how many papers she rattled or boxes she shifted, the moth remained hidden. She understood she should take her sweater with her. She knew about moths, their attraction to keratin. For hours each Havana morning she had read until her tailbone throbbed. Every subject as seductive as the last: French pastry, Persian history, the poetry of Pablo Neruda. But her favorite had been a book on Lepidoptera. She had never forgotten the picture of the White Witch, *Thysania agrippina* in the Erebidae family. In the photo, the moth flattened itself against a pale tree, cleverly blending into the bark. Its wings plush as suede. Its body silky with fur. The size of it had been astonishing, like a dinner plate. Cuba was the land of diminutive things: the zunzuncito, the pygmy owl. In that context, the giant moth had seemed tragically out of place.

So here was her sweater, a thing she greatly valued, and here its enemy. The locker, with its vents and gaps, would offer no protection against such a tiny threat. But Mari left the sweater where it was and shut the closet door behind her—something about that old moth book and her days as a real librarian. *Let it have its little snack.* To a moth such cashmere must be Beluga, not that Mari had ever tasted caviar. Walking home, she even wondered if perhaps there had been no moth. Maybe her eyes were tired from working under those shuddering fluorescent lights each day. Maybe the moth was only a floater. That seemed likely.

⸕   ⸕   ⸕

The heat hit her right away. It wasn't quite as bad as being outside, but the thick air induced a gulping and straining that fixed the librarians to their seats. They patted their faces with tissues they wadded into balls and tossed in the trash, not even rising to recover the ones that missed. Mari looked from one to the other, questioning.

"Now it's altogether broken," Sydney guffawed. "At least we're not cold anymore." The irony was hard to miss, if sickening in the torpor.

Mari shook her head and wondered how long they'd park there—like boulders—waiting. If she were the librarian, she'd be on the phone telling whoever was responsible exactly how it was. No such bullshit on her watch. All those years in Cuba, each day risking arrest—even prison—for the circulation of beauty and knowledge and something so fine that language faltered. What *was* it? A kind of communion, perhaps, between the blood and the page. How many so-called *real* librarians could say as much? Yet here she was now, her only task the mortification of interminable shelving. A library aide, they called her, their absurd chatter about certification and minimum requirements drawing sour saliva to Mari's lips. She could just spit. Los Cubanos were right. Los yumas were crazy.

Used to functioning in heat, Mari slogged through the humid air, opened the closet and put her purse in the locker. *Estoy pinchando*, she thought, *there's plenty to do*, still marveling at the ponderous stones behind the reference desk. *Librarians! They didn't deserve the title.* Her sweater, she noticed, looked rumpled, sort of thick and lumpy, so she smoothed out the wrinkles, clicked the padlock, and set about shelving. On tip-toe, reaching toward the highest rows of books, Mari glanced often at the bright square of the building's single skylight and felt the long line of her body angling for the blue.

In the library, the heat continued for three days. It even made the local news. And each of those days, Mari opened her locker and found her sweater oddly full and plush, as though it were growing. Three times she smoothed out its surface and got to work. It occurred to her that something was the matter with the cashmere—maybe the humidity bothered it—but she took no heed, only running her palms over the exquisite fabric and clicking her tongue as she left.

When the compressors finally roared to life, icy cold rushed in. The librarians said "Ah" and "Yay!" and applauded. But soon it was too cold again, just as before, and the repairmen threw up their hands.

"This is the best we can do, ladies," they said. "It's gonna run cold for a while. We'll keep working on it. Sorry."

The librarians said that was okay. They understood, but Mari wondered what it was precisely they understood. The mechanics of air conditioners? The musings of HVAC technicians? Well, Mari didn't understand. But then she wasn't a librarian, was she? And what sort of a name was Sydney any-way? It reminded her of all those stupid Cubans naming their children after Russian cities—Nizhny, Kazan—or anything that began with a *y* and sounded vaguely Slavic: Yulieski, Yurubi, Yamilka. What relief when the idiotic trend wore itself out and good Spanish names came back into fashion: Estrella, Alonso, or her own name, Mariposa.

Straight as a royal palm, Mari strode to her locker, goose bumps rising as cold air drew the last beads of sweat from her skin. When she could stand it no more, she pressed thin wrists against the pain in her nipples. More ache than joy. More dis-appointment than fulfillment. Somewhere along the way, life had let her down. And yet, she was still too young to simply give up and wait for death. Fingers at the padlock, she paused, held very still, listening. Nothing. Yet . . . *something* was differ-ent. Not a sound exactly, but the air pressure had changed, as if a body not there before was now taking up space. She pulled off the lock and opened the door. The sweater was gone. In its place, a giant moth the magnificent color and texture of Mari's cashmere. A White Witch but bigger. Wings folded, it was about the size of a backpack.

A flutter in Mari's chest made her cough, but she only said, "I see," like she'd expected it, like giant moths were nothing new to her, like even if they were, it would take more than that to unseat her aplomb. Years before, when nearly every-thing she treasured had been stolen—her books, her home, her job, her country—dignity and composure remained, and she'd come to rely upon them. A firm face and rigid spine could feel so much like strength and power.

The moth leapt into the air, forewings pivoting as it lifted, then perched on the wall above her. Gingerly, Mari closed the closet door and cleared a space on some boxes where she could sit down and ruminate. She estimated nearly two feet from compound eye to abdomen tip, and five feet across its fully extended wings. Twice, its thorax subtly pulsed and hind wings flickered. "That's well and good," she said, "*you've* had a king's supper, but I'm freezing, and what'll I do now?" Fussing at it in this way comforted her, and she half expected the moth to talk back, but it only ticked several inches clockwise. Nothing more. "Bien." Mari rocked forward, hands on knees, and rose to leave. But then—gently—it was upon her, embracing her back, fluttering and wafting her hair. She startled. Head ducking, shoulders rising. There was a gasp, even an impulse to strike out, but Mari would not panic, would not be made foolish by an oversized insect . . . or anything else. Ever. So she held still. She waited.

Settling, the moth slid its forewings over Mari's shoulders and halfway down her arms until it looked as if she were wearing a kind of poncho, one made of champagne-colored cashmere and silk. From the back, only the moth's velvety wings were visible, nothing of its eyes or legs or antennae. "What are you doing?" she said. "What are you—" Mari coughed again, but gradually her breathing slowed, her eyes closed, and when she touched it the luscious softness was like down, though she knew from the book that a moth's wings were covered in scales. How long since she'd been held? "You're so warm," she whispered. The dusty closet air changed, became redolent of seaweed and ripe guava baking in the white-hot sun. Mari recalled the fruit's sweet musk from her childhood in Morón, how she'd pined for the jelly-filled torticas at the bakery and had to satisfy her cravings with pilfered fruit from a neighbor's tree. "Okay," she finally said, "if this is how you want to make up for eating my sweater, I'll allow it."

So she went about her business with the moth draped across her shoulders like a shawl, and the librarians complimented the unusual fabric, the complexity of the color, the becomingness of the design. Mari nodded and thanked them, a strange pleasure humming inside her, one that continued well into the next day, when she popped out at lunchtime for a box of sweets to share. It was far too warm for a sweater, but Mari felt quite comfortable walking down the street. She hardly knew how to take it off anyway. When she had returned home the previous evening, the moth released its grip and fluttered to the wall above a lamp, where it remained all night. Its absence left Mari cold and achy. She wished it would change into a blanket and hold her through the gloom. In the morning, when she opened the door to leave, it resumed its position upon her back, and the caress was dulce, made her crave the torticas de Morón she'd missed out on all those years ago.

But in the shop now, she passed over the torticas de Morón, tried not to even look at them. They'd be too sweet, she told herself, though her mouth watered and she swallowed repeatedly. Instead she considered merenguitos, señoritas, coconut pastelitos, all lined up like colorful soldiers. Finally she decided on a dozen quesitos. When the man handed her the change, he asked if he could touch the fabric of her sweater. "Never seen anything like it," he said, his dark fingers skimming her arm, running up to her shoulder, grazing her neck. There was a tingle, yes; Mari admitted that. But those days had passed. She'd been a beauty, and that beauty had brought boys, then men. The men, some of them, had brought trouble and pain that bled into fatigue. Finally, resignation prevailed. Men aged—they were human—but their passions still quivered like caught fish. Their pingas stayed immature and stupid. She'd have no more of that. Better to live with disappointment than the mad frenzy of longing and betrayal.

In their fuzzing sweaters, boxy and unbecoming, the librarians huddled admiring the quesitos, smacking and licking their dirty fingers. They'd never had better ones. "So kind of you, Mari." Sydney smiled and raised her eyebrows as if Mari were a rare bird suddenly roosting on her window ledge.

"Seemed like time for a treat," Mari replied.

"It's always time for a treat as far as I'm concerned." Sydney laughed and patted her belly, shook her head. "I never used to be this way, not until after the divorce. Life. You know?"

Mari nodded and left to finish her own pastry in a strip of sunshine cast by an east-facing window. Outside, the palms whipped, a late tropical storm threatening.

⸾ ⸾ ⸾

That night, when the moth lifted from Mari's shoulders, it flew right to the front door—urgent—thrashing its wings against wood and wall, powdery scales smudging the white.

"What do you want?" A nervous pounding started in Mari's head. Anyone could see the moth was agitated. Anyone could see it wanted out. Mari rushed to the door. If it continued in this way, it would kill itself. Their bodies were so soft, so utterly without defenses. How easily Mari's cat had eaten moths back in Havana. They went down like cotton candy. "Stop, stop!" she cried, and flung open the door, shoved at the screen. Like a ghost, the moth slipped out, paused—as if waiting for her—then stuttered up and over the roof.

Rain slapped the glass and lightning caught the smooth contours of Mari's face. For hours she sat at the front window watching for any sign of it, finally crawling into bed at two. "Can't fly in the rain," she said. "Anyway, I suppose it paid its debt." She pulled her knees to her chest, closed her eyes against the darkness. But the next morning, when she opened the door to leave, the moth rushed in, landed like a fleecy pillow upon her back, spread its forewings down her arms, across her chest. Mari closed her eyes, felt the moon beneath her skin and thought of flying. On her way to the library, she stopped again at the bakery: buñuelos this time.

When night fell, the moth once more beat at the door, once more departed. As before, Mari worried it would not return, and at first, it didn't. But then it came to her on her way to the bus stop and withdrew again after work, even before she'd gone inside her apartment. Soon it came and went sporadically, often near the bakery. Sometimes Mari thought it wanted something from her, that its erratic behavior posed a question she simply could not decipher. When milder days finally set in, she was often without it, forced to explain the odd omission to the librarians, who noticed things like that. Fear of loss gave way to forbearance. Days passed in the moth's absence, then weeks, months. Finally, it was gone. There had been no special parting, no message to help Mari understand the strange interlude. Only a stealthy leave-taking that materialized by degrees, like gray hair.

At the Salvation Army, she sought another such treasure, but there was nothing half so fine. Not even Merino. Just some badly pilled cotton knit and threadbare wool too scratchy even to consider. On the first (likely the only) genuinely cold day of the season, Mari yanked the zipper of a secondhand windbreaker toward her chin and decided to walk to work. *It's done*, she told herself. *Don't give it another thought.* Yet by the time she passed the bakery, she was furious. Wanting in this way, needing to be touched and caressed—like a child or a lover—it made her feel pathetic. If she didn't spit, she thought she might puke, so she stopped at a trash can and, when no one was looking, spit repeatedly into the fast-food wrappers and empty coffee cups.

All through work it was the same: the disgust, the self-loathing, and steadily, beneath the comfort of her rage—such longing. Even before she finished shelving, Mari had decided. She would find the moth, if only to give it a good lashing. Damn stupid freak of a thing! Probably it was a Cuban moth. Only Cuba could whip up such a singular brew of sweetness and despair.

The sun was low when Mari turned toward the bakery. While the man with the dark hands loaded a box with torticas de Morón, she fingered a dish of seashells by the cash register, then went to the window and looked up at the blackening sky, felt the brine of the Atlantic on her fingertips.

"We're famous for our torticas," the man said.

Mari nodded.

"Authentic. Just like you'd get in Cuba. We even make our own guava paste." He eyed her from behind the counter, but she only looked out the window.

"Where's the elevator?" she asked, handing him a twenty.

He pointed to a side door and smiled. "Haven't seen you in a while. Where's that beautiful cape of yours?"

"Gone," Mari said, dropping all her change into the tip jar.

"That's okay." He had dark shiny eyes and café con leche skin. "You're pretty in anything . . . if you don't mind me noticing."

"Makes no difference," she replied, and left.

⸎   ⸎   ⸎

It wasn't the tallest building in Miami, but weather permitting, it commanded a fine view of the city, even a tiny sliver of distant ocean. After the elevator, Mari had walked up several flights and climbed over a rusted gate to gain access to the roof. There, she went to the south side and leaned against the half wall to catch her breath. Minutes passed. When she turned to the cookies, she found the box already open, and swiftly, before doubt crept in, lifted a tortica to her mouth. The first bite tasted bitter, especially when she got to the guava paste that formed the cookie's red center. *Like biting into a heart*, she thought, *the bloody engine of life*. Mari willed herself to chew, to swallow, to finish it, then took another. The more she ate, the better the torticas tasted, the sweeter the guava became. The fourth one she swallowed almost greedily.

"Hermosa," she breathed, and hunched against the chill. A breeze made her eyes water, but then they kept on watering, and Mari didn't know if it was the torticas de Morón, the distant line of ocean, or the stars switching on as the city lights beneath them did the same. Perhaps the prospect itself was to blame: the hope and dread of it.

By the time she started in on a fifth cookie, the moon had risen and there was the moth.

"I knew you smelled like guava." Mari watched the rest of her tortica fall to the sidewalk below.

The moth hovered mere feet away, out in the open air. All its focus was upon her, as though she were the only light in a world turned to dusk. Mari coughed to settle the flutter in her chest—she would be calm—and counted ten whole seconds before lifting her eyes to regard it. At the sight of the moth so near, the memory of its embrace returned with fresh vigor and kindled a burning all along her skin. Not heat so much as rage. Fear. How dearly she would like to tear the wings from its fragile body, steal away with them, wield needle and thread and fashion something indelible to wrap herself in, to the end of her days. To be buried in. But from across the Straits, from Havana, from her old kitchen: words. Neruda: *You can cut all the flowers but you cannot keep spring from coming.*

In stuttering circles the pale moth waited. If it sensed the violence of her thoughts, it betrayed nothing. And at last Mari discerned its question. It seemed to her now that she'd known it all along, that her knowing it was why she was here. Not to destroy the moth or even to lambaste it, but to proffer her answer.

Mari climbed up onto the wall. It was good and thick, so she easily found her footing and was not afraid. Her fingers flexed several times, and she began slowly removing her clothes, tossing them like sails into the night. The cold air struck right through to her core, and against her bare feet the concrete felt like ice, but that was fine. She knew what was coming. Mari pulled her shoulder blades together, drew in her belly, let her head drop back until the Milky Way was all she saw.

The moth alighted. Warm supple tides shimmered through Mari's cells, and the world hushed.

When she lifted her arms, her wings lifted too. When she flicked a pebble with her toes, her hind wings throbbed. She tasted the air with her tongue and looked south toward Cuba, felt it drawing her. *Damn moth*, she thought. The roof of her mouth went cold, and she almost wished she could undo the thing she'd done, change her answer, but it was too late for that. The sky beckoned so deliciously. She craved height and distance, and her body naturally rose, papery wings beating and beating until the box of torticas, the bakery, and all their uneaten sweetness disappeared beneath her.

THE SOUND

OF AVA

So the problem is no longer getting people
to express themselves, but providing little
gaps of solitude and silence in which they
might eventually find something to say.

—Gilles Deleuze

I STILL MEAN TO MARRY AVA. I DO. SHE'S A NICE GIRL,
thoroughly decent—one of those librarians who seem ordinary from far away, then turn out to have skin like a fresh
plane of snow and the languorous eyes of a Sargent. She moves
back and forth behind the counter, swiveling and reaching,
towers of books rising beneath her deft hands. The laser wand

chirps as she fingers *One Hundred Years of Solitude* or *The Art of War,* and you imagine her soft luminous surfaces conceal rare depths of passion. Ava has long, dark blond hair. Natural. Undyed. And she brings me these wonderful sandwiches layered with exotic ingredients: pineapple, kalamata olives, eggplant, some kind of macadamia nut spread. I'm totally off my usual ham with butter. One time she brought me guava paste and cream cheese on a crusty white roll. Can you imagine?

As I said, my plans to marry Ava, to have a life with her, those haven't changed. I'm a lucky man. Really. It's not like I'm all that tall. And I'm not especially handsome. Could be Claude Rains's cousin, though I forget who said so. There's more than looks, of course, but I feel my lack when I'm with her. It's just that—and I only bring it up out of necessity—I never imagined she'd talk so much. *So much.* Like a serene and sylvan wood nymph: that's how she looked to me that first day in her white angora sweater. And even though everyone talks a lot these days, even in this culture of voluminous self-expression, something about Ava's penchant for verbalizing seems preternatural. She flings words about like those people who throw candy at Mardi Gras.

One time, I even counted. Not in a cruel way, not to raise the point with her or anything like that, just to satisfy myself. We were in a bagel shop. My whole order, including the "thanks," took exactly eleven words. Ava used up forty-nine. I don't think I'm especially laconic, but let's be generous and say the exchange might reasonably have required twenty words. Ava was still twenty-nine over that. This means she employed nearly 150 percent more language than necessary. Now think about that level of excess spread across the full spectrum of daily life. That's a lot of words. Perhaps I shouldn't mention it, but even during our amorous interludes, she chats, converses steadily about work, dinner plans, curious turns of the weather. Essentially, she is only quiet while eating and sleeping.

Still, I never really *minded* Ava's verbosity. It was just a thing I noticed. Until recently, I saw it as cute, an unexpected quirk, like a pewter dragon at the center of one of those Russian nesting dolls. But then something odd began to happen to me, at first only occasionally, then with increasing regularity. Now, I must admit an inexorable pattern has emerged, and frankly, I'm concerned. Not in a big-picture way or anything like that. We're still getting married. That's for sure. But the fact is, there's a problem.

♦   ♦   ♦

The first time was two months ago. I waited for Ava in a little bistro in the old market, one of those with dark wood and white tablecloths: diminutive but substantial. Often the first to arrive, I'm accustomed to waiting, so I sipped my tea and enjoyed the mellow babble around me. For some reason the world felt all harmony and beneficence just then. The air cool and dry, everything smelling of woodsmoke and grilled meat. A couple one table over shared a slice of cheesecake and stories from their childhoods. I remember just before Ava arrived I'd been struck by the pleasing way my shoes, socks, and pants lined up: three distinct but compatible shades of gray. Then I saw her crossing the street, floating steadily toward me, her gauzy white tunic delicate as butterfly wings. She is blessed with an inordinate degree of grace, my Ava. I don't mind saying I still feel breathless when she leans over to kiss me, her shiny lips tasting of peppermint.

"Have you been waiting too long?"

"No, no. I've been fine. You're beautiful."

"You're sweet," she said, and kissed me again. I reached for her hand and continued holding it as she ordered, then turned to me with a story. Ava always starts our conversations with a story.

"I felt so stupid today."

"Oh?"

"Yeah, I had acupuncture, you know, at two? And I totally forgot to wear the right pants. What a pain! I wore these tight pants, see?" She raised her leg for me to look. The twill clung to her shapely leg from ankle to thigh. "Anyway, he couldn't get my pants legs up above my knees. He was pulling and tugging, you know, in his low-key all-Zen kind of way, and nothing happened. So I gave them a yank, not my left leg 'cause that calf's bigger, but the right. Sometimes I have this fear that that calf's going to keep getting bigger and bigger, you know? I don't think it is, but I saw that on TV one time. Anyway, I started with the right. I figured I needed some encouragement, and if the right pant leg came up, the left was sure to follow. No cigar. I pulled and pulled, but nothing happened, well, except I got it wedged so tightly onto the thickest part of my calf that I didn't think I'd get it down again. Then I told him, I was like, 'I'm so sorry I forgot to not wear tight pants today—not that I *always* wear tight pants or anything, but I usually remember to wear looser ones.' And you know how he is. Barely a peep. Just a little smile and a nod while I'm sweating and straining to unwedge that pant leg. I finally had to peel them off and put on a stupid gown. At least I remembered it opens in the back. Remember last time I put it on like a coat, you know, with the opening in the front, and he looked mortified when he came in and saw me that way? Like he's never seen boobs!"

So really this was a fine story, and even as Ava told it, I chuckled, smiled encouragingly. After all, she'd captured something of the absurdity of modern life. It was a funny story, even rather poignant . . . from a certain point of view. I like that she's amusing. And it's not as if she wouldn't listen to me if I had a story to tell. I guess what I'm saying is I wasn't in any way annoyed with Ava for telling her story. I think I was even laughing when it happened. The first dagger of pain struck when she said "peep." From there, it swelled into a flurry of knives across my forehead, at the base of my skull. This was no figurative headache. By the end of Ava's story, I felt like I was being lobotomized. What's more, there were lights. Sparking half-moons marshaled at the perimeter of my vision, then began a slow march to the middle. At "stupid gown," I could barely see her face for all the fireworks.

I was just about to explain that I had to leave when our food arrived. Ava busied herself pouring Russian dressing, brushing bread crumbs from her lap, all the while chewing in her delicate way, cheeks rounding with the movement of her jaw. She was enjoying her food. I sipped at my tea, watching her and working out how to explain my imminent departure. That's when I noticed the pain receding, like an ocean wave drawing back into the deep. My eyebrows unfurled. The lights faded. The clenched fists in my head relaxed and flexed agreeably.

"Ah," I sighed, and picked up my fork.

That night, I lay in bed considering. I'd never had a migraine in my life. Even garden-variety headaches were rare for me. On the other hand, I'd just taken a new job, assistant sound editor for a local station, not what I'd imagined I'd do with my life, but film studies majors can't be too picky. Anything with a regular paycheck is a victory. So maybe it was just the stress of the new job that brought on the headache. That seemed reasonable.

But then it happened again, and that's when the worrisome pattern started. I had accompanied Ava to a fund-raising event at her library. Little islands of people chattered among the stacks, types who probably preferred books and cats to human companions but were emboldened just then by champagne and expensive hors d'oeuvres. The room smelled of cheese and mothballs. I can take or leave these things, but honestly, I'll go pretty much anywhere with Ava. That's how I feel about her. A mammoth *OED* displayed on its own pedestal had attracted my attention, and as I leafed through the pages, only half interested in "rickshaws" and "ruination," Ava materialized at my elbow.

"Sorry to leave you alone. I feel like I should socialize with the others while I'm here, though. Everybody freaks out around the donors. Some of these librarians can be so . . . uptight. If I don't do tonight right, I'll get the cold shoulder all week." She guffawed, "I mean, *relax*. Not that I can't handle that personality, you know? Stiff. Stuffy. Am I stereotyping? It just gets"—she let her hands plummet to her sides—"exhausting," and rolled her eyes.

"That's fine." I smiled reassuringly. "I understand." And I meant it. She had to do the rounds. This was her turf, after all. I would not be one of those narcissistic husbands who think only of their own wants and needs, and I hoped Ava realized that about me.

"You're sweet." She smiled. "Do you see that man over there?" She pointed by moving only her eyes.

"The large one with the olive jacket?"

"Yeah. He's a *major* philanthropist. Last year. . . ." And as she narrated her tale of the peculiar donor—his liberal gifts and eccentricities—the pain returned: a searing blade at the back of my head. "He doesn't choose books based on subjects he's interested in," she continued. "He checks them out according to these patterns that change every week or so. One week he only gets red books or gray ones. Another week he wants books with single word titles—*Dracula, Persuasion, Candide*—or only ones that were published in, I don't know, say the 1870s. And what's really weird is he's always wearing these . . ." The words piled up. The pain intensified. I tried to concentrate on the lilting cadence of her voice, the silky white shirt she had chosen for the evening, the glossy mound of her bottom lip, but that's when the lights started. I closed my eyes, rubbed my forehead, and finally Ava noticed I wasn't well.

"What is it?" The note of alarm in her voice comforted me.

"Headache," I managed.

"I'll get you some water." She hurried away, and honestly, it was only a second or two after she left that the pain stopped. And I don't mean it began to ebb. I mean it switched off completely. One second: wincing pain. The next second: *none*. When Ava came back, she handed me the water without a word, the worry on her face urging me to drink. I did and felt better still, refreshed, optimistic.

"Are you okay?" she asked, and that very first word, "Are," was like a hammer to my exposed brain. The pain rushed back, and I needed to sit down. "I know where there's a chair," Ava said, her hand tender on my cheek. "I'll go get it." I had just reached out for the support of a nearby bookshelf when it snapped off again.

"The hell?" I heard myself ask. That's how befuddled I was. Not to mention, the agony had given way to what was perhaps a more disturbing sensation: worry. I had seen the pattern, and my chest thumped at the prospect of the pain returning when Ava spoke to me again.

"Here you are," she said, placing the chair right behind me, and just like that, the headache returned. There were silver starbursts and a ripple of nausea too.

⸭ ⸭ ⸭

After that night, I had to face facts, even facts that made me as miserable as these. Ava's voice, for some entirely inexplicable reason, gave me epic headaches. It happened every time she spoke, even over the phone. That ruled out my smells theory, that the cause was some perfume she was wearing or maybe a new laundry detergent. Even over the phone her words set off a screaming pang behind my eyes. Despondency prevailed. I would lose her. How could I not? She was already growing suspicious of my excuses, the way I begged off first one, then another, then all of our engagements. Of course the truth had to come out. There was no other way.

So one day I swallowed three aspirin, went to Ava's apartment, kissed her hello, and sat down on her sofa. Then I took her hand in mine and explained as gingerly as I could that her voice seemed to trigger a kind of migraine that made me envision sawing off my own head and chucking it into the ocean. But I worded it carefully, each syllable placed just so, like a paint-by-numbers.

Her face went blank. "My voice? You don't like the way I talk?"

"No, I do. It's just the sound of it . . . I *love* the sound of it, but it makes my head scream. *Agony.*"

She thought for a moment, studied me, not even blinking. In the kitchen, the refrigerator hummed. "Right this minute or all the time?"

"All the time, I guess. But I'm sure it will pass. It's just a . . . thing that's been happening lately."

"So my voice is making you . . . ill?" Shimmering in the light from the window, her downy brows rose sharply. How could she not be incredulous? *I* was incredulous.

"Yes."

"Have you seen a doctor?"

"Not yet," I said, struggling with my jacket—where *was* that sleeve?—and making for the door. The pain had switched on, and nausea was threatening, too. I didn't want to throw up or pass out. All the while, I felt her watching me, reading my movements. Losing faith.

"Are you trying to break up with me?" she finally brought out.

"No! Of course not." My hand on the doorknob began to sweat, and I worried that I wouldn't be able to grip it, to turn it and escape the mounting tide.

"Because this feels like a rejection. It feels personal." She fingered a loose strand of hair, glanced outside, shook her head. "Who could believe this?"

"I know it makes no sense. This is wrecking me. I can't lose you. But what can I—"

"No!" Her cheeks had flushed, and somehow that made her look lovelier than ever. "Tell me the truth. *The truth.* It's not like you to treat me this way. vlneH truth!"

"What?"

"reH vaj qabuQ jIHvaD."

"Ava, I can't understand you."

"ghu'vam incredibly hurtful."

This was something new. *The anguish has addled my mind*, I thought. Not only did her words inflict pain, they were growing inscrutable. But in that terrible moment, my hand slippery and grasping, my blissful future with Ava a thinning draft of smoke, it was easy to dismiss the bizarre development. I had bigger concerns. How would I marry her now? And without her, how could my life not become a gaunt and desiccated hollow?

Though I longed to stay, to reclaim my spot on Ava's sofa and explain myself, I couldn't. "I'm so sorry, Ava," I whimpered, "but the pain is . . . I've just got to get away from . . . I'll write you a letter!" By that point, I was halfway down the stairs of her apartment building. Her door slammed behind me, and when I stepped out onto the street, the pain was gone.

Sure, skeptics might theorize that—subconsciously—I wanted to end things with Ava but lacked the courage. A pathetic man devising a pathetic solution. That is unequivocally false, however, and here's how I know. A couple of weeks passed after the awful meeting in her apartment: gloriously headache-free yet gutting, miserable weeks. I wrote her seven long letters but received no reply. Life without her began to seem the only solution, though I often wondered if the emotional wretchedness wasn't worse than the headaches. What could I do? Ava's lovely melodic voice caused me debilitating pain. I couldn't exactly go through life that way. Then something happened that I did not expect.

Other people's voices began to give me headaches, too. The mailman's when I had to buy extra postage for an especially long letter to Ava. The cashier's at the bagel shop. My coworkers'. A group of tourists' on the street. Each word a stab, a bludgeoning. I used up all my sick days, then some I didn't have. Finally, I lost my job.

What's more, their words, everyone's words, began to sound like gibberish, just as Ava's had. Or sometimes I heard languages I didn't understand except to recognize their cadences. There was French, Spanish, Russian, Creole, Chinese, Navajo, even Klingon. I heard a little old lady in the bagel shop say, "raisins muS jIH!"

Her husband responded, "Je sais que pour toi."

My head pounded: the ponderous ticking of a colossal clock. Pores opened and sweat beaded. I was like the man in that old film noir, *DOA*. He's dying but has to solve his own murder before the poison completes its task, so he darts wide-eyed and frantic all over the city seeking clues. That was me. A running man, frenzied and confused, dodging voices and words like bullets, zipping across the street to avoid a couple of neighbors complaining about "honden." I even tried going to the doctor one day, but the exchange with the receptionist nearly blinded me with a screeching white torment that sent me sprinting to the street for relief. Eventually I understood I had to get out of the city. I had to escape the voices. They never stop in the city. In fact, it got to the point that taking public transport would level me. Individual strangers were fine—they didn't talk to anyone. But when there were pairs—friends, lovers, family—it was more than I could bear.

"I'm like, reH po'chugh singing."

"ray' tlr nIS maH!"

"Prefiero patatas."

"Waar is de stilte?"

Soon, it wasn't just voices that gave me headaches. It was all words: emails, letters, books, billboards, even T-shirts with writing. One day I saw a girl in a T-shirt with a single word, CÉLFIE, emblazoned across the chest. I nearly retched on the spot. The lights came on so brightly I considered calling 911 for help finding my way home.

∰   ∰   ∰

That's how I wound up here. Greenland. When I stumbled into the airport that day, as blunted by painkillers and Benadryl as I dared, I had no destination in view. "Somewhere quiet," I whimpered across the counter, wincing. The guy looked at me for a moment, then leaned forward and whispered that someone had just canceled a ticket to Greenland via—it sounded like "Sandwich"—Iceland. I bought it on the spot, thought for a moment, then asked for another.

"Nothing else open for a month," he said.

"I'll take the next available."

Just before the boarding call, I fumbled a last note to Ava, begged her to join me in Greenland, to suspend disbelief and leap with me into the white void. Afterwards I worried the phrasing sounded morbid. I tried to alter what I had written, but the lines of the letters of the words became a little forest of pine trees, so I enclosed the ticket, mailed the lot, and shoved cotton balls as far into my ears as fingers would reach.

The capital of Greenland, Nuuk, has about sixteen thousand people. That's sixteen thousand voices I can easily escape by hiking half a mile in any direction. No equivocating. The town just ends. So, as surreal as it feels to be here, I'm definitely finding what I came for: stark solitude and quiet. The jewel-colored houses of Nuuk did little to prepare me for the austerity of the countryside, and nearly all of Greenland is countryside. Wherever I turn, there is only brown, gray, and white, though at night, the northern lights dance misty rainbows across the sky. This is supposed to be a peak-viewing year, and while we're weeks away from the best date, they're already so beautiful I have to sit down when I see them. Sometimes I lie in my tent with just my head sticking out far enough to observe the sky. My little camp is lonely, though, and I think about Ava as consistently as I breathe.

At first, when the loneliness got bad, I tried my own voice for company. I would whisper Ava's name or the little notes she used to include with the sandwiches she'd bring me. For all her talking, her notes were mercifully (to me now) brief . . . but tender. *I love you*, she'd write, or, *You're sweet*, or, *You and me forever.* But then even my own voice began to give me headaches, and once, when I read, *You're the best*, what came out of my mouth was, "nlvbogh!" Anyway, reading her notes silently gave me headaches too, so I put all that aside, and now I spend my days staring at the sky or hiking and looking out for musk ox. When provisions run low, I trek into Nuuk and buy what I need. Though the locals are friendly, there isn't much conversation. I'm growing a beard and keep my head tucked into my neck. I'm a turtle. Don't talk to me. Thankfully, they don't, much.

It's funny, but out here in the frozen expanse of the world's largest island I hear sounds all the time. Sled dogs, auks, an occasional white-tailed eagle, the wind whisking the barren earth. There's the popping and sizzling of my campfire, too. One night, I could have sworn the shooting stars made slick rushing sounds. None of these gives me even a twinge of pain.

I figure that's a good sign. I'm sure it's just a matter of time before whatever's off kilter in my head settles down and Ava and I can get back together. I still mean to marry her. I hope she hasn't given up on me. Maybe she's rereading my letters right now. Her fingers pale and nimble across the pages, her mouth softening as she warms to the vision of us sharing a glorious nimbus of silence. It might be a relief—this quiet life—not a deprivation. A liberation. If only she'd pack her bags, join me here, I'm sure she'd come to understand that.

⦙ ⦙ ⦙

I try not to notice the passage of time but can't help myself. Like a hypnotized man, pupils spinning, I count every week, day, and now, hour. Ava's plane, if she took it, would have landed last night. Today would be her first chance to come looking for me. Though it costs me great fissures of pain, I write a note to her, make dozens of copies, and leave one with nearly every shop in Nuuk, every hotel, bed-and-breakfast, even the hunting supply store. She need only ask and someone will tell her where to find me. The American with the scruffy beard, they'll say, the odd one who never talks. The turtle.

My tent deadens the air like an anechoic chamber this morning. Only murmurs of my body break through: breath panting; blood pulsing, knocking at my veins until I'm stirring the fire, scraping eggs from the pan, chewing and humming just to ease the pressure in my ears. A couple of auks gambol in the distance, and I balance a bundle of spindly sticks atop my guttering fire. The brittle crackle of their burning is nice. Wood being so scarce, I burn whatever I can find or carry from town. Often I simply strap together twigs and other debris. Low clouds have persisted for days, but the sky is clearing now, and if it continues, the aurora borealis will be spectacular tonight. It's such a relief to view the lights *outside* my head.

❖   ❖   ❖

No sign of Ava. I should eat dinner but convince myself it's early yet, eyes scanning the horizon, snow squeaking beneath my boots as I slowly rotate. Mostly I watch south, toward Nuuk. That's the way she'd come, but every so often I do a 360 just to be sure she isn't staging a surprise. She's clever like that. Beautiful and clever.

Dinner behind me, I survey—for at least the hundredth time—the desolate plane, hear the grind of my teeth, the muffled moan of an anxious man, and lie down in the snow. Faint folds of teal and purple ribbon the darkening sky. Time passes but I stop marking it, have no idea how long I've been gazing, drawn upward, buoyed by a sensation of lightness. *I could transcend this body,* I think, *this ground, this earth. My blood could become air and I could float away.* The thrumming cries of several auks startle me, and I turn to see them rush by, their velvety black heads sleek against the lights, white chests blazing. At the horizon, they disappear, the ocean calling them always back.

That's when I see the polar bear.

Tornassuk, they call it here. Master of helping spirits. Occasionally one floats over on an Icelandic iceberg. This one is surprisingly delicate, probably a female. I'm tempted to call it sylphlike, but surely that's going too far. The ripples of its fur glow in Greenland's interminable half-light. I've heard it's best to make noise in the presence of a bear, alert it to your position, break the odd spell that can sometimes set in. But I can't speak. Won't. Anyway, she knows I'm here. Distance shrouds her eyes, but I can tell by her posture.

The bear moves closer, not lumbering but floating like a ghost or an angel, and that's when I know it's her. *It's her.* Suddenly I'm running, laughing and crying and screaming her name until it sounds like nothing, like gibberish, "Ava! Ava! AvaAv a AvaA va Av a avaavaava!" And she calls out to me then, stands up tall and white and makes a sound rather like my name, but we're too far apart for me to hear it clearly. All I know is she's coming to me, and I'm going to her. Her distant voice bright like a wind chime. Mine a desperate rasp chanting her name. And the lights gleam like blades all around us.

OBRERO

I.

The worker leans forward like he's pushing an invisible cart filled with his own splintered bones. He imagines this sometimes, that all the ways the world has broken him—the long hours, the unpaid bills, the toothache just beginning to throb— have yielded rough gray shards he wheels wherever he goes.

If he'd known the car wouldn't start, he'd have left earlier, in time for the bus, but the walk is manageable if tedious in the dewy grass sogging his shoes. A sidewalk would have been nice.

At the stoplight he waits for the signal and looks at the cars, most of them a glassy black. The color's depth makes the worker think of a moonlit forest, and in it, a dark pool blinking like an eye. Always the same, this reverie: the cool water receiving his naked body, the soft plash, the flattening ripples. He never envisions surfacing.

Among the paused traffic, he spies a face he knows. There is the familiar profile, the turkey swag exposing itself above the collar. It's Mr. Corborant, his boss. Really his boss is Dave, the head custodian, but Mr. Corborant is everyone's boss. Naturally the worker knows Mr. Corborant's face, but is surprised, when their eyes meet, to see embarrassed recognition there. The worker nods, but Mr. Corborant winces—*actually winces*, as if seeing the worker has given him a pain—and looks away, the loosening skin of his neck trembling when he swallows.

♦   ♦   ♦

Morning sun illuminates the tall building's east side. Shielding his eyes, the worker heads for the back, where the custodial crew is allowed to come and go. The walk has worsened the toothache, and he nearly grimaces against the pain. Three hopeful aspirin with breakfast, but they don't seem to be working. There is the night shift, just leaving. And Chico. Black hair, scraggly beard, muscled and shiny, Chico is the color of rye bread, and he makes the worker feel pale and nervous, the way he stares and shakes his head in mock pity whenever they cross paths.

"Morning, guerro!" Chico grins.

The worker mumbles, "Morning," and walks faster.

♦   ♦   ♦

Mr. Corborant is brisk. "Up there." He points to the strobing offender. The worker nods, nudges the tool cart toward the wall, locks the stepladder's braces. He knows better than to speak. Mr. Corborant is a busy man, an important man, too important to chitchat with the day custodian. Anyway, what's a little curtness to the worker? He needs his paycheck, doesn't he? If the boss—even now poking furiously at his keyboard—wants to feel consequential in the collar strangling his turkey neck, let him.

At first the worker figures it's a faraway car engine—that droning sound—so he keeps working. Or maybe something mechanical just outside Mr. Corborant's office: a printer acting up, a vending machine struggling to keep the sodas cold. But when he turns his head, hands fumbling at the light cover and dust floating down around him, he discerns the source.

It's Mr. Corborant.

He's moaning. The noise is primarily guttural but with a thin musical note at the top. It is remarkable how long Mr. Corborant can make this noise without stopping to breathe. All the while, his head rests on his keyboard, the computer bonking madly.

Heat radiates through the worker's chest. *Shit. Really?* Finally he asks, "Mr. Corborant?"

No response.

"Are you okay, Mr. Corborant?"

The worker's arms fall to his sides, the long fluorescent tube above him angling sharply with one of its ends detached.

"The thing is," Mr. Corborant says without lifting his head, the computer still tolling, "I don't feel comfortable with you . . ."—he sits up and glimpses the worker in snatches, like he's too bright to view directly, a flash of cheap sneakers, another of ill-fitting pants, a nose—"the way you are."

The worker fingers a flathead and straightens his back, silently chastising himself for stooping. In frustrated dreams of nefarious enemies, he lopes gorilla-hunched, knuckles punching the ground for bursts of speed that never come. If only he could stand up straight and run like a normal person—even kick out when the mood strikes him. "You need me to come back later?"

"No," Mr. Corborant says. "I mean, these days. Corporations. You know. The cultural . . . *atmosphere.*" He flutters his fingers like the sign for snow. "It's getting to me. I need to focus on my work. Somehow . . . *you're* distracting me."

"I'll come back tomorrow." The tooth pulsates with force as the worker speaks, a spear of pain deep in his jaw, a lacerating echo in his gut every tenth heartbeat.

"*No!* That's not it! I need you to . . . *change.*" Mr. Corborant stares right at him but squints like it hurts his eyes.

The worker lifts the replacement bulb and nods. "I *know.* I can be out of here in five minutes."

"I mean, *yourself.*"

And now, reluctantly, the worker begins to understand. He should have known it would go this way, that in the end, so much would be required of him. He rubs his jaw though it does nothing for the pain.

"You're just—I don't know. How you are. Can you return tomorrow? As a woman? I think that would help."

The worker opens his mouth to speak, waits for words, but Mr. Corborant continues.

"What do we pay you?"

"Ten dollars an hour." Can he take more aspirin yet? He stashed a few in his pocket. Has enough time passed since the last dose?

"Yes! See? That's it! That's giving me acid reflux even as I sit here." Mr. Corborant rubs his chest. "Not much, mind you. I could get over it. You don't *have* to work here. No one's holding a gun to your head. But I'd prefer you took care of the matter."

The worker looks at Mr. Corborant, looks at the dangling tube. "Should I . . . ?" He points up.

"Leave it!" Mr. Corborant rushes to open the door and shoos worker and cart out into the wider office, where rows of heads in rows of cubicles radiate busyness.

◈   ◈   ◈

Once, the worker had had such a violent headache across his forehead and behind his left eye that all the way home he envisioned his eyeball bursting from its socket and plopping on the ground like an oyster. He recalls this now because of the tooth, the pain that makes him want to reach in and wrench it out. And it's probably because of that pain—the way it feeds defeat and fatigue right into the center of his body, the way it makes him long for ease and yeses—that he yields. Even as he wonders if he'll ever again make love to a woman, if he'll be shorter, or weaker, or more prone to crying, he lies down in bed, turns out the light, and yields to Mr. Corborant's words. They cover his body like a warm sheet, like a winding sheet, like a swaddling cloth.

II.

The worker turns to survey her backside in the mirror. It is still a little foreign to her, full and round like this. She thinks of Chico, the way he stares when she passes. Maybe the night crew will have clocked out by the time she arrives. She'd rather be late than walk past those guys, even if she does get docked.

When she bends down to pull on her socks, pain lashes her jaw. She stands up straight, holds still, tries not to drool but can barely swallow as the action forces tongue against tooth. Letting a third aspirin dissolve in a spoonful of sugar water, she worries. Will the tooth fall out eventually? Will it fall out before it becomes abscessed? Before infection invades the bone? Can you die of a bad tooth?

Dew soaks the hem of her pants as she traipses through the tall grass. The car still won't start, and she missed the bus by seconds. The tooth is slowing her down, but so, too, is another, less familiar sensation: nakedness. Amidst the road noise and exhaust fumes, the worker feels exposed, almost as if, despite the frumpy uniform, she is flesh to air. For this reason, she keeps her head down, especially when she gets catcalled. Don't acknowledge them, even in anger. It only encourages them. Isn't that how it works? Engines rev. Brakes scour. Rubber tires tongue gravel and debris. She can barely hear the words, anyway, just scraps here and there: *Me like*, or the banal *Nice ass*, or sometimes she hears *Fuck*, but without context. Such a world.

At work, the night crew has already left, and for this the worker is grateful. Not that Chico isn't handsome. He is, and he knows. He's just not her type. Too vital. Too much personality, always goofing and laughing with the other guys. She bets he has no interior life at all.

In Mr. Corborant's office the worker balances on a stepladder, straining to free the bulb from its socket. The prongs have bent or something and she can barely reach but doesn't much feel like going for a taller ladder. When the tube finally comes loose, she looks it over. One end is black. She suspects a bad ballast but would have to cut the electricity to replace it and doesn't much feel like doing that, either, so up goes a new bulb.

Humming, Mr. Corborant enters carrying a large box, strides to his desk and says, "Ah, that's much better!"

The worker glances down at her chest, the swell of breasts there, the way they push forward for everyone to notice. Nipples even. She'd almost like to tape them flat but imagines that would be painful.

"I'll be able to see what I'm doing again." Mr. Corborant sets down his box with a pat. "Have you ever bought a juicer?"

The worker assumes the question is rhetorical but says "No" anyway.

"Well, count yourself lucky!" He laughs. "I've been trying to choose a model for the last two weeks. Too many options! Pulp. No pulp. Low heat. No heat."

"Anything else?" the worker asks, climbing down, trying to keep her head level so the tooth won't rage again. The aspirin has dulled the sharpest edge.

Mr. Corborant sits, regards her openly, hands coming to rest in his lap. "Actually . . ." He points up to where clumsy scuffs and scrapes mar the ceiling around the light fixture.

"I'll get the paint," she says.

"Oh, and on your way back, could you just grab me a coffee? Cream, no sugar?"

"Sure." The worker feels herself smile and is confused by this. She'd never felt the need to smile at Mr. Corborant before. Naturally, she'd always been courteous, even deferential, but smiling seems excessive. Now the thing blooms in spite of her, like a bruise after the blow. Walking through the office, she determines not to smile again but feels it flash out whenever someone makes eye contact. *Dammit.*

Paint in one hand, coffee in the other, the worker pauses, hears voices inside Mr. Corborant's office. Then Mr. Corborant appears in the doorway and waves her over, reaching for his coffee as she approaches. "We're almost finished," he says, "Chico's taking on a few projects at my house."

Chico nods at the worker, his eyes reflexively sweeping her body.

She smiles (*really?*) in reply, glancing from Chico to Mr. Corborant and back to Chico, but she doesn't care about these men, doesn't want to know what they're planning, what projects, whose house. She only wants her tooth to stop hurting and for Chico to stop staring at her chest. Mr. Corborant, too. When pain and fatigue ebb, other, grander desires suggest themselves, things to do with peace and beauty, maybe a field of borage blossoms, but she doesn't have the energy to conjure them just now.

"Let's grab that contract." Mr. Corborant sets his coffee on his desk and he and Chico bustle out.

The worker climbs the ladder, stirs the paint, dips the brush, strokes over the blemishes. Fumes threaten a headache, but then she is almost done. When the room quiets, she notices the door is nearly closed, only a whisper of office noise getting through. And though she had not observed his return, there is Mr. Corborant, hovering awkwardly near her calves, looking very much as if he has something to say.

"I didn't expect—" he begins. "I thought it would make things easier, but now . . . I feel distracted in a whole new way. Do you know what I mean?" He moves closer. Even through the thick fabric of her uniform, she feels his heat.

"Perhaps we could—do you know the restaurant that's way out on . . . what's that road? Out by the new putt-putt?"

"That's done, Mr. Corborant." Coming down, she turns quickly to avoid bumping into him, fumbles with the tools, struggles to close the ladder.

"I'm as surprised by this as you," he says breathlessly.

The worker hoists the ladder onto her shoulder, sets the paint can on the cart and shoves toward the door, smiling again as she passes him. *Shit. Stop!*

But Mr. Corborant tells her to wait.

She hesitates. "What is it?"

He drops into a chair and cradles his head. Along his part, a silver line unfurls. He dyes his hair. "This won't work either." His words crawl out like a groan. "I thought you'd be—" He looks up at her, and she clears her throat, fully meaning to convey her impatience with this scene.

"You don't *have* to work here, you know."

"I just want to do my job, Mr. Corborant. There's no problem between us." The tone of her voice is placating. She wants to puke.

"Yes. There is. Can you come back tomorrow?"

"I always work Thursdays."

"I mean can you come back . . . you know . . . *different?*"

She has mastered the smile at last.

"Can you come back . . . well . . . darker?"

"Darker?"

"Yes. I'm sure that will take care of things. I'll be able to focus again. This is an unbelievably stressful job. You have no idea what this kind of work is like." Mr. Corborant rises from his seat looking refreshed, even benevolent, helps the worker maneuver the cart into the hallway, and shuts the door behind her.

III.

"Qué dolor!" In the bathroom mirror the worker inspects the swollen gum, wonders if her jaw on that side doesn't look a little swollen, too. She dreamt all night—violent bloody scenes—and feels now as if she never slept at all. But in her reflection, more than the swelling troubles her. She flips the bathroom light off, then back on. Off. On. The light works fine. She is simply dark now—blatantly, immutably dark—and an ugly feeling surfaces, something like diminishment. She rubs nervous circles against her cheek and longs to burrow under the bedcovers.

A glass of milk is the only breakfast she can manage, and most of that she throws up before leaving, too many aspirin taking their toll on her stomach.

From the bus she can see nothing of the dim world around her, only her own reflection in the glass. The jaw *is* beginning to look puffy. In the strobe of passing lights, her hands catch her eye. They huddle in her lap, olive brown and strangely, terribly, beautiful. Still, she pulls her sleeves down to the tips of her fingers. Others on the bus sleep or stare at their screens. This one smiling into the blue glow. That one thumbing like mad. Another one—ah, Chico. Now rising. Now next to her.

"You're too pretty to slump like that," he says, but she has no response. "Ain't this a new schedule for you?"

"Yes." Chico's skin is also olive, but not as dark as hers, and cooler in tone. For a moment, she hates him, wants to ask if he thinks he's better than her. She can barely meet his eyes and stares at the floor instead.

"Por qué?"

"I'm cleaning now, bathrooms, and vacuuming."

Chico moves closer to the worker and settles his voice like they're conspiring together. "You know those projects at Mr. Corborant's house? I've got el jefe so overcharged I can go to Havana for vacation. Want to come? I'll buy you a bikini. Like with the coconuts?" He cups his hands against his chest and laughs, beard bristling.

She holds her cheek, assesses its temperature.

"What's wrong? Toothache?"

She nods.

"Ain't all that cleaning gonna hurt that tooth?"

"Probably." The worker turns in her seat, giving Chico just enough of her back to suggest she doesn't want to talk.

"That's too bad. I got some money if you need to see a dentist. I can help out, you know? I'd like to." He grins, but she only closes her eyes.

"I'm in pain," she says.

"But you smiled at me yesterday. Remember?"

"I remember."

By the end of her shift, anguish is all she knows. She feels queasy again. More than this, she feels defeated, like it would almost be easier to die than to solve this problem: to locate a dentist willing to see her without insurance, to find her way to an emergency clinic and make the case that her toothache has become a medical emergency. She pines for the thick skin of her mother's hand against her cheek, stroking her forehead, the soft words: *Don't worry, mi'ja. Te quiero, mi'ja.* Had it been real? That love? Had there been a life before this one, sensations other than pounding and nausea?

"There you are!" Mr. Corborant calls across the lobby. From his seat on a padded bench, he has watched the worker traverse the whole long space, her black hair glinting silver in the morning sun, shadows nestling beneath her breasts. "I was hoping I might run into you. Your schedule is different. Are you leaving?"

She turns toward him. "Hello, Mr. Corborant." Slurring against the pain, she struggles to keep her jaw still. If she can manage it, she won't even look at him.

"You know"—he rises and walks toward her—"I was observing you just now, watching and thinking. *Wow.* I hate to do this. I mean it. But you've got to make one last change. There's no way around it."

The worker lets her purse—suddenly too heavy—slide from her shoulder to the floor, and for a moment wonders what to do with her hands. They twitch like they would lash out, but then a ringing starts in her ears and she covers her face. The soft chuffing of her breath grows loud in the little cave she has made of her flesh, and she longs to crawl inside it, tuck her arms, and curl her toes until she occupies the only inviolate space she can imagine.

Mr. Corborant lifts his hand several inches, as if to stroke her hair, then sees her breast, the dark rise of it where the neckline dips. The lobby is empty. "Mine," he whispers, and there is the blanched sand of his skin, fingers advancing like a tide. His eyelids droop, and he breathes through his mouth.

At his touch, the worker flinches and steps back, but Mr. Corborant reaches for her anyway. Not urgently. He's not especially aggressive, but his arms are there, in her way as she tries to move past him, fingers fluttering about like moths. Finally he laughs, shoves his hands into his pockets, and shakes his head. "Okay then, make the change."

The worker picks up the purse and rushes toward the door, then pauses to look back at his face, to be sure she understands him.

"Last one," he says, almost tenderly. "I promise. I see the problem now. *Really*. And after all, I'm the boss, right?"

The worker shrugs.

"Hey, no shrugging at the boss!" He wags his finger in mock rebuke, but she doesn't respond. He makes his voice high, cartoony. "Are you even *legal*?" He laughs, then clears his throat. "No, don't answer that! Just make the change."

"Por el amor de Dios," the worker says. Because as much as she would like to be one of the defiant ones—all swagger and swearing—she can't even look him in the eye. She is already as wounded as she can bear, and anyway, her stomach is telling her she'll vomit again soon. So she caresses her own wrist the way she imagines her mother might if she were beside her, nods her assent, and goes home.

Maybe it will be a relief. She'll lose herself again, that's undeniable, but maybe there will also be a boon. *Remember*, she wills. *Remember you are more than flesh of this world. More than a laborer. Remember what you really are.*

IV.

The worker spits out the tooth. All night its powerful tongue poked and prodded, encouraged sometimes by a rush of blood or the splintering of tiny fibers that made its eyes water. Now, there the tooth rests, an ugly misshapen thing already half covered by dirt. But that doesn't quite satisfy, so the worker paws the ground until only grass and earth are visible, then it tries a kick, gleefully casting both hind legs into the sweet morning air.

And the air *is* good—fresh and enticing, the long grass of the shoulder exceptionally fine. The worker eats its fill, then lips a few more fibrous plants as well. Finally it saunters down to the office building, careful to avoid anyone who might be about at that hour. Crossing the parking lot, it encounters Mr. Corborant standing alongside his black car, a spiffy little trailer right behind.

"Ah yes," he says. "Perfect! It's my daughter's birthday this weekend." He starts to lead the worker up the ramp, but it shies and flattens its ears. "Come on now," Mr. Corborant chides, "you need this job, don't you?"

The worker supposes it does and edges up the ramp and into the dark trailer, startling when the door clangs shut behind it. Through wide horizontal slats, other cars come into view, their drivers hunched over steering wheels, gesturing and cursing, passengers staring down at screens. A child looking out her window points and smiles. The worker smiles back in its way, then chews the hay Mr. Corborant has supplied for its brief journey, careful to favor the tender hole its rotten tooth has left behind.

At Mr. Corborant's estate, the worker is instructed to trim the back lawn, guard the house (though guarding things is hardly in its nature), and behave itself when the kids ride or annoy it. It may get wet in the rain, cold or hot depending on the season. It may get lonely. But so long as it conducts itself dutifully, it will have a home on Mr. Corborant's acreage and amongst his children, though they are likely to grow bored with it before the year is up. Already the worker worries about this. When that happens, when newer trinkets turn the children's heads, will the salt lick still be replenished? The water trough? The barley and hay?

Standing in the fulgent green pasture, the worker watches Mr. Corborant drive away. For a moment, silence prevails. Then a banging up at the house, as of a hammer driving nails, draws it closer. There is Chico palming wood, swinging away, a pile of decaying lumber behind him and a patch of yellow like a calico spot forming on the gray cedar porch. The worker brays softly and Chico turns toward it.

"Hey you!" he says. "No trip to Cuba now, stupid. What's the matter with you, anyway?" He laughs and parks three nails between his lips.

The worker snorts and smiles to itself, feels at once naked and invisible. It likes this feeling, considers it something like power to move around in the world unencumbered by clothing, yet unmolested, too. Its hind legs twitch, then spring out, and it tosses its head excitedly.

For several seconds, Chico studies the worker, then takes the nails from his mouth and says, "You're spunky for a change. Why don't you go up to the house and do a little damage? Just for kicks. Get it?" He laughs and moves closer, leans down, his voice airy. "What're you gonna do? Be el jefe's personal petting zoo? *Idiot!* How long will that last? How long before you're a half-dead Humane Society case called in by the mailman? Why not get back at him? Come on—be *bad ass*! Stick it to the man! Go smash that planter over there. Or the door, yeah, bust it down! Screw him, right?" Chico does a little hop and smacks his thigh.

No, the worker thinks, *no, I won't do any of that. Just because you're asking me to do it, I won't*. It makes not a sound but offers Chico the stiff line of its back and dark luster of its phantom eyes.

Setting down the hammer, Chico grabs one of the worker's long ears and begins pulling. "Just break something! You'll like it!" At first the worker resists, but then the pain radiating from the pinched cartilage suggests a better plan.

So it goes to the house, turns itself around, hind legs poised as if to kick out the glass door. But swiftly it turns further, past the door. Legs aimed at Chico. And it doesn't have to be Chico. It could be Mr. Corborant. Maybe the worker prefers Mr. Corborant, but anyone making demands would do. Its spindly legs quake, ready to explode, but at the last it halves the plan, lets only one fire, one sharp piston that cuffs Chico so hard on the thigh he doubles over and drops to the ground.

"You little shit!" he gasps. "*I'm* not the enemy!"

But the worker knows its enemies. It doesn't need Chico explaining the matter. They are many and everywhere. They are Mr. Corborant, yes, and Chico too. They are Mr. Corborant's children, who will ride, then annoy, then abuse it when no one is looking, or perhaps when they are. Cars, too, are enemies, and buildings, and lightbulbs. Also, there is something bigger than this, something more pervasive and abstract that the worker senses but cannot comprehend.

The worker turns its head to see behind, away from the house, a breeze tousling its coarse forelock. At the back of Mr. Corborant's property, a fence, then another, then grassy knolls that lightly mound all the way to the horizon.

Chico, sitting on the concrete thumbing the pain in his thigh, seems to realize what it's thinking, says that it's a stupid idea. "You'll die out there. Eventually you will. How do you expect to survive the winter? What about wolves? What about *food*? Don't your kind need all this special food and stuff?"

The worker keeps staring, its long gray face pensive. The air is redolent and fills its quivering nostrils with something like a memory.

"How often will you see el jefe's ugly mug anyway? I know what I said before, but it's not that bad here. You better hold on to your job, my friend. You and me, we just obreros."

But what Chico thinks hardly registers. Ears forward, the burro hurries to the first fence, whips itself around, fires a swift blow, then another. When that section falls, it canters to the second fence and does the same.

From there the land opens up, reclines on its supple elbows in the brightening sun. The burro rushes forward, its tail switching madly, its belly oscillating as it bobs from shrub to shrub, then to a patch of berries. Bits of green and purple cling to its lolling tongue when it joins its shrill voice to the wild's song and buzz. And the desiccated husk of its former life crumbles. All it senses now is the warm full summer, sugared and beckoning.

Eventually it will cross fields that rise and fall in fertile swells. The sun will grow warm, too warm for some, and the burro will draw near a cool forest where a black pool waits and watches like a dilated pupil. It may stop there, approach the water, lower its head to drink. It may not. Perhaps by then the burro will know the full nature of its blood, the heritage of its dusty race, and journey instead to charred lands where only those hardened by fire can survive.

BUTTERFIRE

THE MONARCHS HAD COME TO TOWN, FLOATING AND tumbling through the air like embers. There'd been something on the news about their migratory route inching westward this year, and now, squinting up over the stopped traffic, Elina regarded them with tears. *You and me*, she thought. *We're a team*, she thought.

It was early autumn but felt like midsummer and Elina's car had no air-conditioning. A stream of sweat tickled her lower back before soaking into the waistband of her shorts. The long line of cars stuttered forward, then stopped once more. When Elina braked, she heard gasoline slosh in the old can her father had given her when she got the car. It struck her that a whole decade had passed since then, and her throat tightened. Pop had been so proud of her, such a smart and industrious girl. All on her own she'd saved enough money to purchase her first car. A good choice, too. Pop said nobody made a more reliable car than the Japanese. He'd beamed for days. In Elina's mind, those final years formed a grim symmetry. One year your father's there with you, smiling like the sun. The next he's sick. By the end of the third, he's gone. Any happy moment, she decided, could be the eve of disaster, and you don't even know it. You just grin and grin. Like a fool.

But the gas can wasn't part of the plan anymore. Maybe Tibetan monks could set themselves on fire, but Elina had decided against it, especially after seeing the pictures. They'd roused waves of nausea deep in her belly, but she made herself look. Absent her own courage to protest in that way, witnessing seemed like the least she could do. One image in particular had taken hold. In it, a monk sat cross-legged and serene as a river pebble amidst the flames lapping his body. Elina had studied his face for signs of terror or regret but found none. And even though that might be construed as a comfort, only a monk, she concluded, could meet such monstrous horror with that degree of grace.

And she didn't really *want* to die. That was a big point to consider. For one thing she was Catholic. Better to live in misery than face eternal damnation for taking your own life. But also, wasn't it too soon to resort to such a final and desolate measure? Yes, she despaired sometimes—even often—but the main trouble issued from one concentrated core: her job. Surely such a defined problem could be solved in a more reasonable way.

Elina's job made her wretched. Tired. It kept her poor verging on destitute. It demoralized her. She'd had it with the daily procession of smugness, of condescension, or worse, of refusing even to see her. That was the cruelest offense. Astonishing how many people grabbed their chips, paid for their salads, asked where she was hiding the cream without looking at her once. *Not once.* She might as well have been a robot . . . or a mouth. She could have been a disembodied mouth for all they cared. Them with their six figures. As if a shitty salary and ugly cafeteria uniform made you invisible. Some days she wanted to scream at them: *You're gonna die, you know!* Not like a threat, just a fact. *Nice clothes and shiny cars don't make you immortal, dumbass! You're not magical emperor of the timeless universe.*

She'd had it, but that wasn't the same as embracing death.

Elina glanced at the instruments of her revised plan: the plastic bag of browning bananas on the passenger seat beside her, and next to it, a bicycle chain, padlock, and handcuffs. In the back, a jug of orange juice well past its prime. How long would she go to jail? A few days? A month? And maybe after, she could write a memoir or something, go on some shows. People would finally *see* her, see how beautiful she was, and smart, how excellent her English, how hard she'd labored year after year only to flounder in unyielding poverty. Most of all, they'd see how *wronged* she was. They would pause for a moment in their tailgating, and shopping, and eating out, and traveling, to share the burden of her indignation. Her moral outrage. Maybe someone somewhere—someone not invisible—would even dare to demand change.

Once, when her father was young and had had enough, he had marched into the office of the company president, said his piece, ripped off his shirt in one sweeping whoosh and cast it down upon the president's desk. The tiny clinking sound of buttons hitting hard surfaces filled the awestruck pause. "There!" he said, with a snort. "Isn't that what you want? The shirt off my back? I give it to you freely!" Elina wished she'd been there to see it. When Pop told the story, he emphasized how the man's eyes had bulged, the most frightened blue eyes Pop had ever seen. Elina wondered what the company president had said after her father left his office. Did he bend down and pick up the buttons from Pop's shirt? Maybe he ordered his secretary to do that.

Leaning her head out the car window, Elina felt the sun on her face, watched as thousands of monarchs flapped clumsily against hot banks of air, then relaxed into the easy glide that rewarded their labor. It was almost imperious the way their black silhouettes blotted out the sun. "You're a bunch of rebeldes Mexicanos!" she called out, and laughed. The news said the monarchs were on their way to Piedra Herrada, where they would spend the winter. Elina almost wished she was going with them. What a bother all this was: the traffic, the hot car, the loco plan that would probably end badly. Maybe if she returned to Puebla and once more breathed the cool thin air that had first filled her lungs, she could start her life over. She had no memories of the place where she was born, knew it only from her mother's cuentos and a little tin of fading snapshots Ma kept in her bra drawer. Still, Elina could swear it called to her sometimes.

But Elina really knew only this town, this hot, flat, midwestern college town with its shit jobs and millionaire coaches, its big causes and awareness-raising. Well, what about *her*? What about a decent wage and some sick days? A little dignity? Why couldn't *she* be somebody's cause? What about not killing the delicately glowing soul inside her, that trembling entity that quaked as often with fear as with the energy to shoot like a star across the sky?

The old car's brakes squeaked as Elina rode the gridlock. If only the brake pads would make it another month, just until enough money had been saved to change them. Or would she be in jail a month from now? What happens to your car when you're in jail? Do they save it for you somewhere? Two butterflies tumbled together like lovers, and beyond them, the silver glimmer of an airplane. For a moment, jet roar overwhelmed the street noise, and Elina wondered where the people inside it were going so sleek and fast. Resentment washed through her. It might be inconceivable to the people who hurried through her line each day, but it *was* possible to get trapped in a town, to literally lack the means to flee.

What was all the traffic, anyway? Another football game probably. Or a high school basketball tournament. Did those happen at the same time? She never could keep the sports seasons straight. All she knew was one sport or another always unfolded with astonishing self-importance. A happy, hot-doggy, beery energy electrified the air.

Elina considered her breasts. They were central to the revised plan—the one without gasoline and death. High, round, dark. She knew they were exceptional. She remembered skinny-dipping once and all the guys congratulating her boyfriend when she peeled off her bra. She had that effect, even now at thirty-one. One small power to wield against so much indifference. This part of the plan would mortify Ma and Pop, but Pop was gone and Ma was far away. And her breasts would create such a delicious stir. At last, people would *see* her. More than see her, they'd fear her as the self-satisfied always fear aberrance. How glorious to watch alarm supplant those smug expressions. That gratification alone would make whatever happened after worthwhile.

Fuck you all, she thought, dreamily.

Because when hope flagged, she hated them—the smug ones—hated them in a way that made her feel sooty inside. She hated hating them. Tried not to. But she couldn't help it.

So many sins to name at her next confession. She'd better *not* die, not with those on her soul.

From her car's tinny speakers, a commercial insisted something or other would be rápido y fácil. Lies of course. Nothing was quick, and nothing was easy. Everything, in fact, was hard. But Elina was up for it. She would have her day. They owed her that. She straightened her spine, prayed, crossed herself, and turned up the music. It wasn't her style— old-fashioned accordions pumped over a relentless polka beat—but at least it was Spanish. The words comforted her. She wasn't even nervous.

❦   ❦   ❦

On campus, dense clusters of gold gilded the plain air. When they fell into shadow, their wings darkened to orange, then black. Just as they'd said on the news—the biggest kaleidoscope of monarchs in years. Like delicate fires all around. Elina had about half an hour to prepare before the midday lunch swell. Even in the heat, outdoor spaces would fill quickly, and she'd chosen a tree along the main sidewalk to attract the largest possible crowd. Until the police showed up.

When she bent over to retrieve the orange juice, her nose ran in a thin clear stream, so she went to the back of the car for a paper towel. Probably the effect of too much adrenaline. Wiping her nose, she felt her hands shaking. Nerves? Now? Well, they would pass once she got going, once her body synchronized with the day's singular tempo. A moment's impulse made her grab the gas can before closing the hatchback, and from the bottom of the glove box, a book of matches. Best to have options. Something like a gun you pray you'll never need. Anyway, more than human flesh burned. Tires. Trash cans.

At the tree, Elina set down her supplies and strained to breathe normally. Every inhalation seemed to lodge in her tonsils. The plan was to douse her naked body with fermented orange juice, chain herself to a tree, and wait for the butterflies to land—hundreds of them, maybe thousands. Eagerly, they would lap the sugar from her skin. The spectacle would be striking, like fire but sweet, the opposite of death and destruction. No more arrogance. No ignoring. No condescension. *She'd* be the one with power this time, the power to disrupt. Elina had thought the whole thing through and found it satisfactory in every regard. Already, the butterflies flocked to the offerings of banana she'd set out.

✦ ✦ ✦

No matter how she pulled or angled it, the chain would not reach around the tree trunk. That was the first problem. Without it, how could she secure herself to the tree? Just feet away, a cluster of blankly expectant faces watched, waited to be entertained, figuring, perhaps, she was a kind of street performer. Elina looked around for a smaller tree or a pole but saw nothing promising. A tiny panic began pulsing at her temples.

"Can we help you do something?" someone offered.

Elina shook her head, thinking. Should she disrobe or first find a replacement tree?

"What are you doing?" Another voice from the crowd.

She shook her head again.

"Are you a protester?"

Elina wished she'd made a cardboard sign to forestall such

questions. She had a speech prepared—words like blades, she'd labored over each one—but it wasn't time yet.

Loath to upset the gathering monarchs, Elina decided to stay where she was and undress. She set her eyes somewhere just above people's heads, let her vision go blurry, and began unbuttoning her shirt. Then she slid off her shorts. She had intended to be totally naked for her protest. She'd seen those Ukrainian women, and the ones in Brazil. Bold. Brave. Angry. Women who understood how to demand attention. But now, in the light of day, with so much ordinary chatter around her— cell phone chimes, a breeze ruffling the dry leaves—naked felt like too much. She removed her bra but left her underwear on. If only she'd known it would go this way. She would have worn gray underwear or black. Not these with their little owls with hearts for eyes. Not these silly ones.

The crowd grew. Someone gasped—nothing so disorderly as nudity in broad daylight. A few applauded—probably mocking, or ogling. There would be photos later. But then a woman with frizzy gray hair and concerned eyes came right up to Elina and placed a hand on her arm. "Are you okay?" she asked. "Do you need help? This doesn't seem safe."

Elina nodded, tried to smile, swore silently not to cry. "I'm doing what I've come to do. It's okay." She glanced up and drew courage from the monarchs circling above, sensed their collusion with her plan. Soon several more women approached, then a couple of men, too, all softly cooing their concern and support. But this wasn't what Elina wanted. She'd come to make a statement. She had a plan. All she needed was a little time and space. *These people needed to give her some space.* Where were they before it came to this, anyway? Where were they last winter when she went without heat for a week? Or at the end of each pay period when the only food left was beans and rice? When she couldn't even put gas in the car? Weren't a few of them the same complacent assholes who strode through her cafeteria line each week? Who worried openly about airport delays and where to board their expensive dogs while they vacationed in Iceland? *Now* they were concerned for her? Something about their tight-lipped half-smiles and whispered solicitude irritated her right to the brink.

Elina raised her voice and thrust out her hands: "Get back!" Everyone moved away from her then, and though that was her intent, something in their faces made her angrier still: the shapes of their eyes, the lines where their lips pressed together. They weren't alarmed, weren't awestruck. Yes, they looked at her, but with a sickening patronage. Here's what it was: they saw her as a *case*. A patient in need of treatment. And in this way, they maintained their position above her. They were sane. She was not. They were well. She was sick. Like you'd have to be crazy to protest in this way? Wasn't the exploitative system the thing that needed fixing? Wasn't *it* sick?

Someone in the crowd whispered, "Police," and Elina remembered her time was limited, particularly since she wasn't chained to anything. The cops could easily show up and drag her away. She grabbed the gas can and poured a thin but wide circle around the tree, wide enough that the limbs wouldn't catch even if the flames leapt up, wide enough that the monarchs could safely reach her inside of it. The ground in that area was too much dirt and sand to readily advance a fire, anyway.

Elina knew enough to allow the vapors to dwindle before igniting a flame. The powerful smell made her cough as it was. When she finally held the match to the strike board, the crowd stumbled back. Someone called, "Wait! Stop!" Her hand shook, but she struck and flicked the match to the ground. A flash of orange raced the circle, then settled into a low border of flames, the crackling fire and cries from the crowd all running together. Elina smiled. *Now* there was alarm. But there was no real danger. She wasn't stupid. She'd hardly used any gasoline at all. The fire wouldn't last long.

Elina walked to the middle of the circle, lifted the vessel overhead, closed her eyes, and drenched her body. The initial coolness felt sweet against the warmth around her. Someone screamed, though Elina couldn't imagine why. As the liquid dried to a sticky pungency on her skin, she kept her eyes closed. Voices—urgent, indistinct—swelled and broke over her. Far off, sirens stirred the hot air in wide plaintive arcs.

Right away, Elina knew what they were—the ticklish sensations along fingers and shoulders, knees, and breasts—the tiny tapping of butterfly wings, feet, tongues. They had come, just as she knew they would, fanning, and tapping, and licking her flesh. They had enveloped her, set her ablaze like the glorious creature she was. Who dared regard her now with anything but awe? Elina let the splendid vision in her head fade and opened her eyes to a world golden and trembling.

CINERAMA

AT THE HARDWARE STORE, SHE BOUGHT THREE FULL-length mirrors and a bag of French burnt peanuts. The mirrors were the biggest they sold. OVERSIZED, the sticker said, twenty pounds each. For this reason, they did not fit in the shopping basket. Getting them from the store to the car took three trips, and she should have worn better shoes. The Florida summer made her flip-flops squishy, toes sinking in, sensing the hot asphalt beneath. She stutter-stepped around stringy blobs of gum. From somewhere in the parking lot, Bob Marley drifted, his voice casual and cool, telling her not to worry 'bout a thing.

But Neva did worry.

She wrapped a beach towel around the mirrors and stacked them in the trunk of her car. The peanuts, still cool from the store, were slightly stale, but she ate them anyway and stared through the windshield at the cumulus clouds piling for a storm. When Neva was little, her father pointed at a stack of clouds just like that and convinced her they were mountains in the sky. Granite and snow, he had said, suspended by magic. He squatted down to her level, one hand on her back, the other tapping her belly as he talked. Above their tiny forms, the blue dome of space just sprawled.

Halfway home it began to rain, but it always rained in the afternoon. That was no reason to change her plans. By sunrise tomorrow, the sky would clear over an empty beach, with only waves and gulls to cut the silence. Was it possible she'd need more than three mirrors? Maybe six would have been better, or even nine. She slowed in the downpour and turned up the wipers. Three would be hard enough to lug out past the dunes. They would have to do. It was a senseless idea anyway. Neva knew it was unlikely to help, but she had to try something. It was frightening to be disappearing in this way. Maybe it came with age—she was nearly fifty—but where did it stop? Five nights out of seven, that question worried her awake.

When she felt hopeful, Neva viewed the problem as more of a fading than a disappearing. Still bad but with a less dire end point. Disappearing could only conclude with extinction. Fading, on the other hand, suggested a lessening, and Neva had long accustomed herself to less, recalibrating again and again to accommodate newly diminished states: fewer parents, less money, fewer friends, less energy, less beauty, less power, less joy.

Explaining the situation, even to herself, proved difficult, not because the words wouldn't come but because she didn't understand what was happening. When Neva stood before the medicine cabinet each night or flipped open the visor in her car, she found in her reflection the usual things, but they failed to make any *impression*. Was she old or young? Lovely or hideous? Kind-looking or foul? In style or frumpy? Did she look like a peasant? Smart? Slow-witted?

I look like nothing, she kept thinking. *Nothing at all.*

Brown eyes, two ears, a chin—the individual elements were clear enough, but when measured for effect, she looked to herself like the following things: a Kleenex box, a box of cornflakes, a cornflake, a cardboard toilet paper tube, a paper bag, dry toast, gravel, a sidewalk, a tin cup, and dryer lint.

◈　　◈　　◈

Neva leaned the new mirrors against the front door, next to the cooler she'd fill with water and snacks in the morning. Then she set the alarm for 5:00 a.m. and lay down in bed.

When the fading had begun, she'd felt the need to move closer to her reflection, to climb inside herself and ferret out the thing she'd lost. She bought a magnifying mirror and envisioned the beautiful and not-so-beautiful women for whom it was intended, women with hopeful eyes and aging skin, young women with acne or skin smooth as silk. Sitting in a kitchen chair, a square of natural light raining down around her, Neva held up the magnifying mirror and studied herself: a field of hairs, pores, bumps, and tiny scars. She imagined women laughing and commiserating over their grotesquely enlarged faces, but Neva felt nothing. At close range, she didn't even look human.

Neva shifted onto her back and stared at the ceiling, waiting for sleep. Her mind roved ahead to the coming day, the early drive to the beach, the mirrors lined up.

Two weeks ago, one o'clock in the morning had found her flipping channels until she settled on a peculiar film from 1952: *This Is Cinerama*. A revolutionary new cinematic technique, it said: three synchronized cameras, 146 degrees of vision, nearly as panoramic as the human eye. A roller coaster crested a rise. Pyramids of water skiers swerved and grinned. Neva had sipped her chamomile, enjoying the scenery. But then the voice-over said, "That feeling of reality!" She leaned forward in her seat, set down her tea, and wrote his words on a notepad.

Reality sounded promising, especially when, where Neva's face should be, the mirror returned a bedsheet worn to the point of transparency, ghost of a ghost. *This Is Cinerama* took the widest view possible. Perhaps that was what Neva needed: herself in context, the story of her in the world. Maybe then her face would find its way back.

So she had stuffed the magnifying mirror in a junk drawer and stood as far from the bathroom mirror as possible, shoulder blades brushing the hallway wall. The image cut off at the thighs and was still bland as tube socks.

Downtown, there was an old department store with exceptionally good mirrors, big clear ones at the end of a long runway that bisected two rows of dressing rooms. Neva had grabbed a handful of tops, some of them with ugly gold sparkles, but never tried them on. Instead, she walked up and down the runway: a tall, olive-skinned woman with long hair and black eyebrows. When the saleslady asked how she was doing, Neva said, "Fine, just taking stock." The saleslady said she "totally understood" but looked as if she didn't.

Outside, glass storefronts widened the view, but the reflection grew dim and shadowy. She was barely distinguishable from the people hurrying to lunch or window-shopping. Sometimes she blended with mannequins posing jauntily in their new clothes. If anything gave her away, it was the eyes: dark saucers of fear, and for all that, still bland.

◈   ◈   ◈

At 5:00 a.m., Neva rose with the alarm and peeked through the bedroom blinds. The bright moon sat low on the horizon portending a clear morning, so she packed two cream cheese and guava paste sandwiches, took Windex to the mirrors, loaded them in the car, and headed out. Empty streets made the going easy, and that cast a halo of rightness over her plan.

The quiet brought everything so close: the ticking of the blinker, the brake pedal's bump and sigh. Every time she swallowed, the sound rushed at her, and the world along with it. It gave the sensation of being in a movie. Neva sat at a red light and watched several cars roll through the intersection, thankful for the road noise. She had caused a car accident once, not that it was her fault. At twenty, in a summer dress and sandals, she'd walked along a busy street on her way to class. A man in a truck swung his head out the window to watch her stride and rear-ended the car in front of him.

Her fingers at ten and two squeezed the steering wheel. They looked old, crinkly, but then she raised her left hand, turned it palm up, back over again, and thought it looked rather young. And her pants: the way the linen ballooned at the knees when she straightened her legs suggested the fabric concealed not a flesh-and-blood woman but plain air. Then the light turned green and she rolled toward the sun and ocean.

Neva had begun noticing her invisibility to others years ago, the way they saw right through her. She came to view herself as someone whose death would be deemed premature but not particularly tragic, and each passing year would only worsen the problem. There had been a college student on the news, a good-looking guy with curly black hair tearfully lamenting the death of a friend. He said, "He was just too young," and shook his head. Then he said, "It's not like he was fifty."

Neva had considered his words a long time, formed many rebuttals in her mind. Everything clings to life, she had wanted to tell him. Cows, sensing slaughter, make a break. Spiders skitter away just before the shoe. Seventy-five-year-olds enroll in experimental drug trials. Neva felt no less tethered to life at forty-eight than she had at eighteen. Even one hundred years is a terribly short time to spend on an earth so old and so bound for a fathomless future. Calculated as odds, the fact that we are here on this planet at the same time, sharing this wisp of history, makes the difference in our ages meaningless. But she'd kept these retorts to herself.

Anyway, Neva could handle social irrelevance. She could handle being deemed inconsequential, not worth looking at. None of that was any fun. At times it had upset her, but she could handle it. What she couldn't handle was holding up a mirror, expecting her familiar face, and finding only a row of soda crackers.

By the time she reached the coast, a sliver of sun had crested the horizon. Puffs of smoke-gray clouds, their bottoms pink as coals, loitered while the sky powered up. Crossing the Intracoastal Waterway brought back day trips with her parents: her father's dark fingers balancing a cigarette as he drove, ribbons of her mother's hair fluttering out the open window, and from the tinny radio, easy FM blowing through the jasmine in their minds. In the backseat, Neva sometimes colored or drew, especially when the drive was long. More often, she searched the dazzling ocean for dolphin fins.

For now, it looked as if she had the beach to herself. The flat waves would keep surfers away, and the only other early birds were solitary shell hunters: old women, turtle-hunched, who seldom looked up, and not even they had arrived yet. Neva hoisted her bag onto her shoulder and tucked a mirror, towel and all, high up under her arm like a surfboard. Brittle sea oats rustled along the boardwalk, and her flip-flops flicked sand against her pants. When she'd come here as a child, Neva had wanted to make a bouquet of the sea oats, but her mother explained how they were protected and couldn't be picked. This was protected land, one of the only remaining stretches of Florida coastline not colonized by condominiums.

Far above, a pair of silvery seagulls hovered, their webbed toes splayed like they were coming in for a landing, though they never did.

"I have nothing for you," Neva said to them. "Don't even think about my sandwiches."

She'd imagined setting the mirrors up along the dune, where it broke into the beach. In her memory, this break had been steep, like a three-foot grass and sand cliff that met the beach at a ninety-degree angle, but that was wrong. The dune's soft shoulder sloped gently into the beach and would provide nowhere to lean her mirrors. She should have bought poles, six of them. How stupid of her.

The mirror had begun to slip, so she found a smooth spot, set it down, laid out her big orange beach towel, and dropped her bag onto it. Then she went back for the others, carrying two this time. When her arms began to burn, she glanced down at the swell of her bicep and hoisted the mirrors higher. She even stood holding them a few seconds longer than necessary, then squatted slowly and laid each one next to the other, all three in a neat row.

Puffing a little, she rested her hands on her hips, blinked

against the brightness, and glanced around for something to prop up the mirrors. Driftwood? A broken beach umbrella? Half a surfboard? Nothing in sight.

Neva exchanged her pants for shorts and donned the big frumpy hat she hated. Walking the water line, she tried to focus on the shells, the ephemeral sheet of glass with which each wave glazed the shore. But the thought would come: *I am ridiculous. This is ridiculous.* Even her toes felt embarrassed, the way they gripped and wrinkled with each silly step. How satisfying it would be to bury them in the sand.

In the distance: a gnarled bundle of driftwood, like skeletal fingers, reached skyward.

By the time she dragged the branches back to her spot, a couple of shell hunters had materialized. No matter. Neva dug holes with her hands to anchor the branches in the positions she wanted and leaned the mirrors against them. They had to be arranged in just the right way. In 1952, they called the shape a "smile box," so named for the bowed format of the viewing screen designed especially for Cineramic films. This meant the two outside mirrors angled slightly inward. All three mirrors lay on their sides, forming a wide rather than tall reflective plane, and Neva peeled off the glued-down plastic frames so that nothing would impede the reflected image. *Please*, she thought, *I need to see myself.*

Each time the angles seemed like they might be right, she hiked down to the water to assess the setup, then trudged back up to nudge the mirrors left or right, higher or lower. The task required many adjustments, but finally the mirrors enabled Neva to see herself from a great distance. Only up close would the view narrow, concluding at the last with two sets of sandy toes.

When the mirrors were in position, Neva sat down on her towel and ate half a sandwich, tossing the other half to the gulls after all. For several moments, the screaming, flapping violence of their appetites owned the morning. Then the brutes sailed away as if their hearts were made of gossamer. Neva drank a bottle of water. Look at those women, those shell-hunting women, their whole focus on the pearly treasures before them, heedless of the savage Atlantic lapping their heels.

She lay back on her towel and closed her eyes, unclenched her fists, counted backwards from a hundred. Perhaps she was fading away, but her senses still perceived her body: the violet water blending with hot cotton blending with guava blending with sweat. Her breathing as loud in her ears as the waves. Last night's insomnia spread drowsiness through her limbs until her feet pointed out, like a ballerina's in first position. Between her fingers, sand clung. When she sifted them, it almost hurt.

"Well," she said, slapping her thighs and standing up, "let's have a go." Her voice sounded loud and unnaturally jocular. She put her hands in her pockets, drew an N in the sand with her big toe. "Okay," she said, nodding.

Neva walked down to the water and pattered through the clear wash, stepping around several crab holes. Then she turned and spied the speck of herself in the mirrors. She took off her hat and waved it to make sure that the reflection was hers. A blip of white wagged like a blown hibiscus. Hat back on.

At first, she only stood there taking in the dot of herself. Nothing. No revelation. But that was okay. The process needed time to play out. "Now, walk," she said, but not too fast. And relax. Try catching yourself unawares. She sauntered, snatched a bit of seaweed and tossed it. Just when she thought her guard might be down, she looked hard at the distant figure of herself, something like a hatted clothespin moving ever closer. Behind her, the foaming waves mounted one on top of the other, and several gulls ran a footrace through the shallows.

Except for Neva, each element of the scene plotted a wide horizontal line: the blue sky/green ocean horizon, the dashes of white waves, the demarcation between the water and the wet brown sand, then the dry white sand that composed most of the beach. Cutting through it all: a woman. Far away, she could have been young still, twenty-five or thirty. She was lean and long limbed, her hair thick and wind whipped. The flat disks of her knees wheeled beneath her skin, legs lifting high as she negotiated the soft ground.

When she drew closer to the mirrors, the hair that had looked dark from a distance glinted silver, and the skin of her neck slightly rumpled just below the chin. At the last, she had to stoop to keep her face in view. Black lashes. Two lips. A nose. There it all was—about as affecting as tree bark.

Back down she went. One of the shell hunters glanced her way, and Neva waved, but the woman did not wave back, kept up her slow walk along the shore. Instead of letting her arm fall, Neva blocked the sun with her hand and wiggled her fingers. They looked big and dark, definitely opaque, and from behind them, the sun's bright aureole blazed.

This time, Neva walked parallel with the mirrors and, rather than attempt to catch herself unawares, openly studied the figure moving back and forth. Again, it made no impression, evoked no feeling or thought. Except for the L shape where the ankles became feet and the hands like spatulas, it barely triggered recognition. Just like looking at a paper plate.

Neva ran, skipped, lay down. She did twenty-three jumping jacks, stripped to her swimsuit, then put her clothes back on. The shell hunters might have thought her odd, but she'd come for an answer. It made no sense to demur now. When she found a smooth egg of blue sea glass, she ran as fast as she could to the mirrors, then crouched down to witness her face in the flush of its small joy. For an instant, Neva thought she glimpsed something meaningful: the color in her cheeks, the black seeds of her pupils, the beach flung wide behind her. These things flickered through her mind like false starts, like when you think you're about to remember something important only to feel it slip away again.

In the dull aftermath of that spark, Neva sat down in the sand, a bit of detritus waiting for the tide to change. She ate her other sandwich, watching herself chew and swallow. Eating amplified the lines around her mouth as well as the dimples she'd had all her life. Her father, when she was little, had called her his "dimpled darlin'," and she had rolled her eyes but secretly delighted. She studied those dimples now. They looked like two dun pebbles.

Eventually, she lay down once more on her towel and pulled her hat over her face.

She would not cry.

◈   ◈   ◈

An awareness of someone drawing near roused Neva a moment before she felt the pain in her shin: a pressure, then a scraping. Someone yelped, a female voice making an "Ah!" sound, and Neva looked up to see one of the shell hunters, a woman shaped just like a bowling pin, tumble into the mirrors. The crackling, splintering noise was awful.

Neva gasped and hurried to her. "Are you okay?"

Having landed on her front, the woman rolled over, sat up, and examined her knees, her hands. "I think so." The voice was thin. "Bruised dignity and a little cut is all." She pressed several beads of blood rising on her palm and shook her head. "At least I've had my tetanus booster!" This with a laugh. Then she looked at Neva. "Is your leg okay? I'm sorry, honey. I didn't even see you there."

"It's fine," Neva said, brushing sand from her ankle, glancing back at her orange towel, the lurid beacon of it.

The woman leaned forward on her hands, struggling to her feet. Neva grasped her fleshy arm and lifted. "I was intrigued by those mirrors," the woman said. "Trying to figure out what they were for." She looked at Neva expectantly, cheeks flushed, white hair sticking out on one side. She looked like a widow, like a grandmother, like a shell hunter. That was the look of her. Was it everything or nothing?

"It's just a silly experiment, not worth explaining," Neva said. The middle mirror had been badly mashed, with most of the shards adhering to a cardboard backing. A few winked from the sand. The other two mirrors had only shifted, rectangular pools of perfect blue sky.

The woman laughed. "It's a *lot* of mirrors!" Then she reached around to brush the sand from her backside.

Neva swept the woman's sleeve, where her shoulder had driven in. The fabric felt warm, and she wondered if it was because of the woman's blood heat or the sun. Maybe both. The woman patted Neva's hand, said, "Thank you, honey," and as she did so, Neva caught herself in one of the mirrors. Her lips were pink, and she looked as if she might be wearing eyeliner though she wasn't. The sun glinted gold along the bridge of her nose and across her forehead. Where the breeze moved the curtain of her hair, her long neck curved into her shoulders. Same features as always, but lovelier, fuller. *There I am!* she thought. *It's happening.*

The face suffused her senses. Like wind chimes. Like sofrito in hot oil. Like pineapple cake. Magnolias. It vibrated like a lizard on a leaf. It morphed. There it was freckled and smiling between her mother's cool hands. There was her cheek squashed to one side as her father, smelling of smoke and Old Spice, kissed it. There were her sixteen-year-old eyes with too much makeup. There they were decades later, puffy and red. And there she sat watching *This Is Cinerama*, blue-lit, the hollows of her cheeks exaggerated in the half-light, her black eyes shiny and haunted. For those few seconds, her face bloomed before her. Familiar. Rare.

Then it was gone.

The shell hunter gave Neva's hand a last squeeze and trailed down the beach, each step a careful little project. The wind picked up, was turning cool, and Neva rubbed the goose bumps on her arms. All about her, and within her, the tyranny of irrevocable things.

⫷ ⫷ ⫷

Neva wrapped the broken mirror in her beach towel, folded it in thirds, and slid the lot of it into the trash can by the parking lot. She considered mashing the remaining mirrors—the satisfying crunch and crackle—but instead put them in the trunk of her car and walked down to the water line. The waves arced higher, churning up green tendrils and coating the shore in murky spume. Soon the surfers would come. And the families. Boogie boards and striped umbrellas would clutter the beach, high-pitched children and lean men in wetsuits claiming it all. The shell hunters would disappear.

But not yet.

A common cockleshell made a little dam against the last rivulet of a receding wave, the sand sliding into a V around it. Neva picked it up and rotated it. No chips or cracks, so she slipped it into her pocket. A bigger wave roared past, the water lifting to her knees, bubbles fizzling all around.

What drama it was right now, like this. What panoramic splendor, this seascape: rapacious gulls and old women the only actors.

SPOT THE

STATIONS

I WANT TO SAY IT STARTED WITH SPOT THE STATIONS. THE app. Have you heard of this? They alert you every time one of the three space stations will be visible in your area, provide the angle too: forty degrees, sixty. Then you rush outside at the appointed hour—eleven thirty at night, three in the morning, it varies—and gape like a child at that bright point whizzing by at 17,150 miles per hour. Only my abuelita knows this, but I choke up every time.

I *want* to say it started with Spot the Stations. It didn't. It started with birdwatching. We'd be having another outbreak or super typhoon, an apocalyptic wildfire—understandably, it'd be all anyone talked about, but still—and I'd squirrel away in Caballo State Park. This was evenings, weekends, summers, and winter breaks (breaks being the best thing about teaching high school). Me listening and craning for a new bird to catalog: eastern bluebird, migrating snowy owl. Recording a new sighting in my little book gave me a boost, I guess, but it also felt kind of silly after a while. For me personally, I mean. Around here, most birdwatchers are older women. White. Middle-class. And nothing against them, but I'm young, male, and Latino. Also, I grew up poor. Damn poor. Eviction-notice poor. I told my family I was hiking all the time, but I wasn't. I was birding with Sharon and Darlene, who were both widowed, depressed, and sometimes baked me cookies.

One day in woods lead gray and patchworked with snow, I had a revelation. A Williamson's sapsucker—rare find in this area—hopped along a branch. I understood right away what a big deal it was. As a birdwatcher, I should have suppressed a whoop of joy. Instead, like I didn't think much of its special yellow belly, I returned my gaze to the legions of Canadian geese overhead. It looks like they're sailing, but they're really flapping like hell. That's when I realized the only birds I cared about were the high-altitude fliers. In migration, Canada geese maintain about 3,000 feet, but they've been reported at 29,000 feet. Over Africa, Rüppell's vulture flies as high as 37,000 feet, the same height as commercial airplanes.

For a while, I stalked geese, hawks, vultures until my neck seized, but soon I abandoned birding altogether and moved into a high-rise apartment. It felt good up there, thrust into the sky like an obelisk. I greeted falcons at eye level, and the lunatic world of humans looked inconsequential beneath me. Like toys: the crawling cars and tiny toots of their pathetic horns, the pinheads moving around so importantly. Seemed like they couldn't do any harm if they tried. Ha.

When I wasn't teaching social studies, I basically lived on my balcony. Ate dinner out there, usually something microwaved—lasagna or burritos—I shoveled in to sate my hunger, then I'd knock back a beer, my eyes tracing the routes

of birds, clouds, airplanes. During the outbreaks, medical heli-
copters buzzed by like dragonflies.

In this way, years passed. I kept teaching high school, kept
hating it. Sorry. Teachers are supposed to love their jobs, bleed
for their kids. One of the illnesses proved fatal only in adults,
so we all kept going to school, saying the kids don't get seri-
ously sick, so, yeah, duty. It never seemed to strike anyone as
cruel to expect teachers to die for their jobs. Not to mention,
they're not all "great" kids. Teachers like to gush—*such amaz-
ing kids*—but everyone knows some of them are shits: spoiled,
entitled, lazy, bullies. Just like with adults: lots of good ones,
but a handful are genuinely terrible people.

Anyway, I kept teaching because . . . what can you do?
Latinos work hard, rarely complain, except to each other.
That's our thing, I guess. Kept watching the sky too, aching
for altitude. I moved to a taller building, imagined leaping
from my balcony and soaring away from all of this, rising and
rising until distance hid the earth in a gentle mist. Abuelita
says people who stare at the sky all the time are obsessed with
God. I don't know what I'm obsessed with, but I do know I
want out, and I wish she could go with me.

So, one night, totally by chance, a space station slid into
view, the brightest star in that moonless sky. I stood up. Had
to. Three in the morning felt like the city holding its breath.
For a whole minute I tracked it: this tiny square of light that
tinged pink just before disappearing. It was crazy to think
there were people in there, that right at that moment they
were maybe eating brownies or putting on socks. That's when
I signed up for Spot the Stations. I've spotted them hundreds
of times now, can even tell them apart.

But here's the exciting development: officially, I'm going.

If I keep living with my abuelita, hoard money like a miser, and, at the end of five years, sell everything I own, cash in my retirement, and take out a personal loan, I'll be able to travel to Blue Station. You get to live there for a whole month. And they have this diversity program that subsidizes part of the cost, which I would definitely need. I hear it's competitive, but Abuelita thinks I'm a good candidate.

Can you imagine? The expanse? The silence? The smallness of this wrecked world? And maybe at the end of my month, when it's time to go back, I can hide out somewhere. Maybe they won't notice my absence and depart without me. Solar-powered electrolysis produces oxygen indefinitely, and the water is recycled. The station's store of freeze-dried food would sustain me for the rest of my life. And other than waving to my abuelita—which will sometimes buckle my knees with weeping—I wouldn't even look much at the earth.

SATELLITE

LATER, IT SHOWED UP IN THE PAPER, A BLURB JUST beneath the photos of face painting and corn roasting. Like it was more than a weird rumor. Like it was fact. As if a woman could up and walk to the moon on beams of light.

�◈◈

They had come for the funeral only to find the town of Mortimer, Arizona, festooned for an autumn festival. Everywhere you looked, orange crepe paper shuddered in the breeze. It gave the impression the whole place was on fire. Smoke, too, hung about the trees, suggested, when inhaled, roasted turkey. Posters hawked three days of corn mazes, beer gardens, funnel cakes, all beneath the biggest harvest moon in decades. They had not come for a festival. Death drew them to Mortimer, but Julie didn't mind the coincidence, not so much for her sake as for her mother's. The fussiness of it all would please Joan. That thought somewhat eased the clenching in Julie's stomach.

It felt silly bumping along in that way, a thirty-two-year-old woman in the backseat of her mother's boyfriend's Chevy Malibu. Karl and his big belly at the wheel, Joan in the front passenger seat staring through the glass and murmuring little ohs of surprise at every new thing. Rhythmic as breathing, Julie thought: *Here I am. Here I am in this car.*

"Hope they've got caramel apples," Joan said, her voice loud and toneless. "I could go for one of those about now. Whatcha say, Karl? Gonna buy your girl a caramel apple?" Joan turned to wink at Julie, who mustered a laugh.

Karl grunted and steered them into the hotel parking lot.

⚜   ⚜   ⚜

In the restaurant, Julie kept envisioning herself from her mother's perspective, not that Joan seemed to give much thought to Julie these days. It was obvious that she—no other way to say it—found her daughter boring now. Julie knew this mostly because of a recent argument, one of only a handful they'd had in all their years. What happened was Joan had sold all of Julie's *Star Wars* action figures at a garage sale, said she was cleaning house to make room for a workout studio. Julie said Joan could have asked, that she knew how tiny Julie's apartment was, no storage and all. And right out of the blue Joan said, "It might be the modern age, but that doesn't mean I have to be happy about a thirty-two-year-old single daughter with no life!" Words like a tiger bursting from its cage.

Later, Joan tried to explain how mothers count on certain things—reasons to buy new dresses and get their hair done. It's hard on them when they don't materialize. "You don't know what that's like," Joan said.

So that she wouldn't be always on the verge of nausea,

Julie had resolved to laugh off her mother's disappointment, to shrug every time she recalled it, but she gnawed her fingernails anyway. It grew increasingly stressful just being around Joan, as if the flatness of Julie's life—yes, she conceded there was flatness—were an injury she'd inflicted upon Joan personally. She'd not meant to be dull. She'd not meant to be alone at thirty-two, but then what was thirty-two? It wasn't old. She just needed to get out more, take up a hobby, maybe find a job she liked. The bank had interested her at first, but now . . . all those couples filing in to apply for home loans. Sometimes they even got there before the bank opened and pressed their faces to the glass. What tedium.

"They've got twice-baked potatoes, Mom. Your favorite." Julie patted Joan's back encouragingly and pointed to the plastic menu.

Joan said, "What are you having, Karl?"

◊　　◊　　◊

After dinner they set out for the fall festival. Joan still wanted that caramel apple, and Julie was grateful for the loops of white lights and tinkle of bluegrass. Mother and daughter sifted through trinkets for sale, Karl following behind. There were macramé plant hangers and pinch pots and shoes made of hemp. In a particularly quiet moment, Julie asked Joan to tell her about Uncle Roy. She'd wanted to ask since the news of his death, but it was hard to find the right moment. All through the two-hour drive to Mortimer, Joan had chronicled the lives of neighbors who'd gotten married or divorced or sick. She went on at particular length about her boss firing her for not knowing computers and wouldn't he regret it. Though

she'd heard much of it before, Julie nodded and made affirm-
ing sounds but found no opportunity to raise the subject of
Uncle Roy, who was dead now.

She wondered what he'd been like. Was he happy? Did he
have any family or friends? She'd heard he'd died at home,
well, in a rented bungalow. That could have been okay pro-
vided he wasn't alone. She hoped he'd not been alone when
he died.

Joan fingered a doily, her yellow hair fluttering in the cooling
breeze. "Divorced," she said. Then also, "You know brothers."

But no, Julie had no brothers, no idea what that meant.
She pressed for more. Joan put the doily back and picked up
a refrigerator magnet. "I don't know," she said, "Roy never
stayed put anywhere. He wasn't what you'd call reliable. Kind
of a loner. But he was funny." Joan had liked this about him.
"Always cracking everyone up!" she said. Julie knew Roy only
from a handful of Christmases and photos, but he'd never
struck her as especially funny. He had sallow eyes and stood
with his hip stuck out to the side, as if holding himself upright
were a lot of trouble.

Julie lifted a glass chili pepper toward the setting sun, and
a red glow flickered over her face. Talking about Roy in this
way gave her hope she and Joan could be closer than they
were. Wasn't that a thing? Funerals bringing people together
by reminding them of their shared mortality? Maybe, by
degrees, Joan could find Julie interesting again. Julie reached
out to tap her mother's arm, to show her the glass pepper, but
Joan had gone to Karl, was showing him the magnets she'd
found, cooing over details only they could see, the subject of
sad funny Roy behind her. There came to the daughter then,
just out of reach, the sharp edge of a feeling—something like

insubstantial or *sheer*. But it never rose to the surface. Even if she'd wanted to, Julie couldn't have named it or plucked it away like a splinter.

❖　❖　❖

"So, Miss Julie." Joan smacked her lips at the caramel apple's stickiness. "I've got an idea."

Inside Julie's ears, a fullness bloomed.

"How'd you like one of my old beaus?" Joan darted a mischievous look at Karl and grinned. "I've got quite a few. Let's see, there's Davis. He was the one with the wife in a coma. Remember?"

Karl navigated the thickening crowd, Joan and Julie following in the open space just behind him. Julie prayed for silence.

Like a vocal exercise that began on a high note and slid down, Joan said, "Oh shoot," filler words for when something tickled her. She began counting on her fingers. "Then there's Tom. He looked nice in a pair of jeans. I'll tell ya that!" Here she nudged Karl, who only shifted a toothpick to the other side of his mouth and paused before an especially smoky food truck.

"Might pick up one of those brats," he said. "Those smell too good to pass up. Want a brat, Joan? Jules?"

Julie said, "No thanks," applied peppermint lip balm and raked her hair away from her face. From a distance, she'd make you think of granite, solid like that, but sometimes she looked down at herself half expecting her hands to float away or to find her legs made of cobweb.

Her mother forged ahead, up to five now, but then she broke off and clapped her hands. "Look! They're having an Elvis impersonator!" She pronounced it "owl•vis."

"That's Johnny Cash," Karl said, nodding toward the poster, reaching for the mustard. "Don't you know the difference?"

Joan wasn't listening. She'd found a table of colorful papier-mâché heads for sale: chicken heads and cat heads, horse heads and bear heads. Whole heads hollow inside with cutout eye and nostril holes.

"You wear 'em," the woman explained.

"What are they for?" Joan asked.

"Just for fun. I put sawdust in the papier-mâché. It makes the heads real strong."

"Oh Karl, look at the horse! I *want* it!" Joan positioned the long horse neck above her head and began to slip it over. Julie thought it looked more like a dog than a horse but didn't say so. Then a swell of music from across the street drew her away from her mother. Three old-timers played the fiddle, guitar, and mandolin. People had begun to dance, among them a tall girl with dark hair. She wasn't exactly a "girl," maybe twenty-five, but "woman" didn't seem to apply yet. Julie crossed the street, the song swirling like a dust devil all around her, the girl turning, too, skirt flaring. She was more striking than pretty, with thick eyebrows and dark olive skin. Like a boat at sea, was how she moved. Julie admired that remoteness, the way the girl closed her eyes, as if the rest of the world had evaporated.

But then a man was dancing with her, twirling and laughing, almost—but not quite—mocking. The girl slowed, barely moving as his arms reached toward her, his long fingers finding her rib cage, thumbs pressing just beneath her breasts. Every bit of her stiffened. When she walked away, he followed, both of them halting near Julie.

"Hey, I just thought we'd have a little dance. I didn't mean any harm. Can I buy you a beer?" He smiled a wheedling smile.

"No thanks."

"Oh, come on. I been here all my life and I never seen any-thing like *this*." His hand threaded the air, indicating the full length of her body, even grazing her hip with his fingernail. "Be still my heart, right?"

She said nothing.

"Awww, why you being this way?" Still with the smile, his back round, his pelvis slouching toward her.

She turned to go, but he followed again, both sets of feet grinding gravel. Four paces, then, in the middle of the street, she wheeled around, looked fully into his eyes, said, "Seri-ously?" and walked away.

Hands on hips, narrow chest rising and falling, he stood staring after her. Like a thing barely worth doing, he forced a laugh from the side of his mouth, then shook his head as if anyone could see he'd been wronged. When he passed Julie, a choking odor—of sour beer and cigarettes—traveled with him.

Julie turned and rushed after the girl, looking back once to make sure the man wasn't following. She didn't know what she intended to say, but she hurried right past her mother, who was shimmying like a stripper. Muffled giggles escaped Joan's new horse head, but the neck was too long, and it made her look strangely tall. Joan's own eyes and nose couldn't possibly align with those of the horse. How could she even breathe?

Scouring the crowd, Julie finally spotted the girl, and before there was any chance of chickening out, walked right up and asked if she was okay. "I saw what happened," she explained. "That man."

The girl half smiled and said, "Same old," but her fingers shook when she tucked a strand of hair behind her ear.

They moved aside so amblers could pass. The girl—her

name was Rebecca—asked if Julie was going to the "moon thing" later.

"The what?"

A few miles from town, Rebecca explained, some rich eccentric had built an interstellar light collector—a giant wall of polished parabolic mirrors that concentrated moonlight into beams of lunar energy. It was one of only two such devices in the country, maybe the world. People came from all over just to experience it, she said. She had come from Miami.

Rebecca had the blackest eyes Julie had ever seen, pupil and iris all the same color, and her gauzy clothing wafted patchouli every time she moved. Julie decided not to mention that she had come for a funeral. Best not to speak of death just then.

"They say it's euphoric in the moonlight," Rebecca went on, "like being underwater or in Heaven. *Healing.* People come out changed, like their depression's gone or their eyesight's better. This one woman was bald from stress, and all her hair grew back!" She glanced up at the sky.

Julie said, "Wow," and Rebecca laughed.

"*Exactly.* Want to come? There's a van soon. The best moonlight's between eleven and twelve tonight."

Julie thought of her mother and hesitated, but there was that edge again, that shard of something rising. And there were Rebecca's eyes looking at her, staring right at her.

"Okay," Julie said, "for a little while anyway."

"Good." Rebecca squeezed Julie's arm like they were old friends and laughed. "You know you look just like a Pre-Raphaelite painting? Can I say that? Those women with their pale hair and gray eyes, strong jaws? The Roman nose? That's you. You're a Pre-Raphaelite beauty. Bet you didn't know!"

Julie's neck went blotchy.

"Don't look so stricken." Rebecca laughed. "Just say 'Thanks.'"

"Thanks."

⸬   ⸬   ⸬

Near the papier-mâché heads stall, a small crowd had circled someone lying on the ground. No one spoke, but Julie heard a rasping sound, regular as a heartbeat and loud. Someone was sawing. Then a hand shot up, Karl's hand waving Julie over. The crowd parted enough to let her through, and that's when she saw Joan on the ground, a paramedic sawing off her head, really *digging* into his work, the muscles of his right arm flexing. Joan moaned, but not the way you'd think someone would moan when they're being decapitated. Perhaps Julie should have rushed in, stayed his hand, flung the bloodied weapon away—there *was* blood—and saved her mother's life. But she froze. Stood staring. Barely daring to breathe or blink. Something about the moment struck her as delicate.

Saw, saw, saw, went the blade. "Oh, oh, oh," moaned Joan inside the horse head, the papier-mâché softening with the friction of the hot metal, pinking from the blood.

"The head is very vascular," the paramedic said, panting, wiping the blade with a white cloth. Julie widened her stance, felt as if she were swinging in tiny ovals.

Karl's voice: "She got it stuck."

"She did?"

"*Really* stuck. I pulled as hard as I could and fell onto those chicken heads back there." He pointed to a fresh red scrape on his elbow, then to a pile of mashed chicken heads on the ground. Tonguing a toothpick, he nodded toward the paramedics. "They're doing a good job, but they nicked her scalp. See the blood?"

Julie nodded, watched the man saw off her mother's head, felt her breathing align with the wheezing of the blade. She checked the time. Rebecca would be waiting. *Hurry*, she thought.

"Is Julie here?" Joan's muffled voice called out.

Julie startled at the sound of it and for a moment considered ducking away, signaling silently to the crowd to keep her secret. Instead, she said, "Yeah, Mom, I'm here. Are you okay?"

"Oh, I'm a tough old bird. It'll take more than a horse head to keep me down."

The crowd laughed. Julie told her to hang in there and glanced at the horizon, at the bit of yellow moon peeking over.

Finally, applause as the paramedic peeled away the last fragments of papier-mâché. There was Joan's face smooth as a boiled egg and streaked with blood and sweat. A small cut marred the hairline, and surely there'd been some oxygen deprivation, but she struggled to her feet and bowed for the crowd.

She would need stitches and a tetanus shot. Joan, sitting on a gurney holding a gauze pad to her head, turned toward Julie and laughed limply. "Well, here's a story to tell, huh, kiddo? What my crazy mom did at the fall festival! Oh shoot."

Julie smiled, shook her head as if Joan were an incorrigible child. "But you're okay now, right? I mean . . . it's just a few stitches. Do you need me at the hospital? Karl will be there." But as soon as Julie said it, she could see it would never work. Joan looked hurt, her mouth going slack in that way she had.

✦   ✦   ✦

In the waiting room, Karl crunched through a bag of corn chips, and Julie sat in a plastic chair staring out the window. Not angry—that wasn't it. Not hurt, because what sense would that make? Mostly she felt incredulous. Bad timing, was all. Here, at last, was a chance at something. She couldn't say what. Maybe it had to do with Rebecca's black eyes looking at her, maybe with that interstellar light collector. Maybe the moonlight would even change her. She'd like to be changed, wouldn't she?

Behind her, Karl struggled to open a second bag, potato chips this time. "Small portions," he grunted.

Julie cupped her hands against the glare. The moon had finally risen, and it was just as Rebecca said it would be— radiant as an eye looking and looking down upon you. Who were the Pre-Raphaelites anyway? She'd read some of their poetry in college but knew nothing of their painting. She'd have to look them up when she got home. Julie let her forehead drop against the cool glass and whispered, "Shit."

Only two patients in the tiny emergency clinic: Joan and an elderly man eating chewable aspirin from a paper cup. He sat in a wheelchair parked in the hallway. From somewhere nearby, Julie could hear Joan, plain and loud. "Yep," she said, "but I'm a tough old bird. No horse head's going to ruin my fun!" Then came laughing and Joan saying, "Oh shoot." She seemed to be having a good time.

In the dim and empty clinic, Julie went in search of her mother, though she couldn't have said why. To comfort her? Prove her worth as a daughter? Or maybe a different motivation drove her. The joy in Joan's voice, the mirth—it was maddening. They'd come to Mortimer for a funeral. Uncle Roy was dead. Had Joan forgotten?

Up ahead, a square of moonlight found a dark patch of hall-way. When Julie passed through it, she thought, *I'm a satellite.*

The voices grew louder, more distinct, and then it sounded as if Joan were crying and calling Julie's name. "Oh, Julie," she said. "Oh no!" Julie hastened forward, breathing fast. *I am coming,* she thought. Around a corner and there was Joan, just visible through the gap in a set of curtains not fully drawn. She sat on a cot laughing so hard tears streamed down her face.

Julie poked her head in and said, "I heard you call my name, Mom. I'm here."

"Oh," said Joan, "I was talking to *this* Julie," and gestured toward the nurse.

"She's expecting a baby," said Joan excitedly, "and her husband likes the worst names you've ever heard. Listen to these—"

But Julie spoke over her, words like bricks walling out her mother and this woman's husband's list of meaningless names about which Julie didn't give a shit. "I'll be back," Julie said, but even then wondered if she meant it.

By the time she got to the lobby, she'd made up her mind. "Karl," she said, "I've got to go. Tell Mom, okay?"

"Okay, Jules." He held out a potato chip. She took it and tasted the salt.

⸙   ⸙   ⸙

At the festival, stragglers gorged on half-priced hot dogs and fifty-cent nests of cotton candy. Hollow voices reverberated in the emptying streets, and some booths were already shuttered. The moonlight made the town look bald and pitched long shadows along buildings and cars. Julie searched everywhere for a sign, a poster, anything about the interstellar light collector. Everyone she asked had heard of it, but no one knew about the van. Overhead: the winged silhouette of an airplane—no, an owl.

But then she saw it: a crowd loading into an old van. Heard it: "Last boarding call," someone yelled, "to the moon!" Then laughter.

Julie hurried over, calling, "Wait!" and a woman wearing a papier-mâché bear head held the door for her. "You all going to the interstellar light collector?"

"You better believe it," the bear head said.

Julie paid her fare, then stared out the window as they bumped along the county road. In the van that smelled of popcorn, with the funeral looming, a decapitated mother, and Rebecca and the moon waiting just ahead, nestling down felt especially nice. A sturdy wind rose outside and the trees' black bones reeled against the still-brightening sky.

※　　　※　　　※

It looked like a drive-in movie theater, but instead of a screen, a wall of mirrors mounted improbably from the desert. Great shafts of reflected light angled down where tiny human figures undulated in a lake of moon glow. Julie thought it would be golden, but the light actually read bluish gray, then blurred into navy where it met the night. Artificial, was how it struck her.

She walked toward the field and saw Rebecca right away, a gently rotating shape whose skirt and hair briefly floated, then flapped wildly when the wind surged. Now that she was there, Julie felt awkward about the whole thing, thought of going back to the hospital without even saying hello. She paused, began taking tiny steps in reverse while watching to be sure Rebecca hadn't seen her. But Rebecca did see her. She smiled and waved Julie over.

"I'm glad you're here!" Rebecca leaned in for a hug, seemed pleased. "You've got to experience this. It's surreal." She pulled Julie to the far end of the field, away from the others, from the parking lot and the little building where you could get coffee or a vending machine snack.

"My mother . . . she got hurt, but she's fine . . . probably mad at me." She followed Rebecca across the sand and gravel, imagining her mother's expression when she found Karl alone in the waiting room. "I guess I shouldn't stay long."

"That's okay. Just hold out your arms for a minute. Feel the light on your skin. Feel it touching you." Rebecca stopped walking, put out her arms, closed her eyes, and began to sway.

Julie shouldn't have come. Whatever she'd expected, this wasn't it, this with the swaying and the touching. It was all kind of weird. Julie looked up at the giant moon, the dozens of silver mirrors radiating light down around them, the blue sparks it made of Rebecca's hair. She tried to close her eyes as she'd seen Rebecca do at the dance, but they kept springing open, seeing all these people. A few hippie types gamboled about. Others stood shifting their weight from hip to hip, lifting their arms for occasional inspection, like sunbathers. What were they doing here? What problems were they hoping to put right? What miracles to obtain?

When Julie turned back to Rebecca, she spied her about thirty feet away, hugging a guy whose tan hand rubbed little circles against her lower back. They rocked in unison, their feet lifting in perfect synchrony. Of course, a girl like that would have partnered with someone. Maybe they'd buy a home together, come to Julie for help securing a loan. Maybe they already had a home together.

The wind kicked up.

Julie sat down then, right down on the ground—as though her bones had gone wispy at last—and drew her hair into a fist until the wind settled.

"You okay?" It was Rebecca.

"Tired," Julie said.

"Yeah. I could take a nap in all this moonlight. Maybe if it weren't so cold. Do you want to get coffee with us?"

"No thanks. I'll stay here for a bit."

"This is Caleb, by the way. Doesn't he look like a young Johnny Cash?"

Julie nodded. He did, actually.

"Catch you up later?" Rebecca's eyes looked a little bit sorry.

Julie said, "Sure," and watched Rebecca's tall form stride into the darkness. Then there was her own body: hands, thighs, knees, feet. A feeling flushed through her, something like embarrassment, but she pushed past it. *Here I am*, she thought. *I am here.*

It was tempting to get up and go. Grab the first van back to town, find her mother, apologize for running out like that, make everything normal again. Instead, Julie laid herself on the baked ground, and her vision glazed. The crisp edges of things melted. Time passed. Minutes. More. Or maybe time didn't pass at all. Maybe it stopped. Goose bumps stippled her arms.

Uncle Roy, slumped and sallow, floated into her mind. Sad, she decided. Could never have been funny, not really funny anyway. And he'd died alone. Julie knew it. A long-divorced man with no children, moving through the desert like a tumbleweed. Probably her mother knew it too and didn't want to tell her. Probably everyone figured she'd wind up the same way.

Julie put out her arms and sensed the planet's gentle spinning. The light was brighter than she'd have imagined possible. Almost like sunlight. She slapped her hands against the dirt and felt the layer of rock below it and the molten core beneath that. *I am a satellite*, she thought, *and this is my earth.*

When she was ready, Julie stood up, the whole world a blaze of white.

⫼   ⫼   ⫼

From a distance—to the curious loitering near the little building, the people dancing in the glow, to the festival attendees still awake at that hour, still laughing in their cat and bear heads—it looked like a woman climbed up onto the moonbeams and walked into the sky. Of course, it was an illusion—with that giant moon casting weird light and shadow like spells upon the earth—but that's how it looked.

Acknowledgments

THE IRONY OF ACKNOWLEDGMENTS PAGES IS THAT, TO those who author them, the words feel inadequate. This is my inadequate attempt at thanking all those, without whom, there would be no book.

I am grateful to (and for) my agent, Wendy Levinson, whose warmth, immeasurable wisdom, and willingness to champion a story collection have amazed me. I am also enormously grateful to Helen Thomaides at W. W. Norton, again, for taking a chance on a collection, and for her editorial virtuosity and humor throughout the publishing process. My book is infinitely better because of her. Thank you to Amy Robbins for (superbly) copyediting this book, and to designer Grace Han and art director Ingsu Liu for its striking cover. Pink and green always remind me of the Florida of my youth. I am incredibly honored that my debut work found a home at W. W. Norton, the press that published the first book I ever bought. Thank you to everyone there who worked on this project.

Many thanks to every editor who first published these stories in literary magazines. I am particularly grateful to Sacha

Idell, Tom Jenks, Phong Nguyen, Alexander Weinstein, Adeena Reitberger, and Erin McReynolds, all of whom, I suspect, taught me far more than they know.

While I hold no degrees in creative writing, I am grateful to all those generous souls who know more than I and freely share this knowledge. Special thanks go to my early mentor, Raul Palma, for all he taught me as well as for discovering that I seemed to be writing a collection. I am likewise grateful to Rachel Cochran for her keen eye and kindly candor. And for their years of generous support, advice, and encouragement, I thank the brilliant Joy Castro and Timothy Schaffert.

For their excellent research assistance, some of which made its way onto these pages, I also thank Maddie Stuart and Rachel Stein.

For her years of enthusiasm and encouragement, I thank the fantastically talented Valery Varble.

And though I come to them last, I thank my beautiful family most of all. Without their love, support, encouragement, levity, and incisive feedback, I'd have little to say and no inspiration to say it.

Muchas gracias, all.

About the Author

BORN IN FLORIDA, IN THE SHADOW OF CUBA, PASCHA SOTOLONGO is an award-winning author and professor who teaches creative writing and literature on the Great Plains. Her fiction has been published in *The Southern Review*, *Narrative*, *American Short Fiction*, *Pleiades*, *The Normal School*, and other venues. When not working and writing, she dreams of the ocean.